Resume Speed
and Other Stories

D0815716

More by Lawrence Block

COLLECTED SHORT STORIES

SOMETIMES THEY BITE • LIKE A LAMB TO SLAUGHTER • SOME DAYS YOU GET THE BEAR • ONE NIGHT STANDS AND LOST WEEKENDS • ENOUGH ROPE • CATCH AND RELEASE • DEFENDER OF THE INNOCENT

NOVELS

BORDERLINE • GETTING OFF • RANDOM WALK • RESUME SPEED • RONALD RABBIT IS A DIRTY OLD MAN • SINNER MAN • SMALL TOWN • THE GIRL WITH THE DEEP BLUE EYES

BOOKS FOR WRITERS

WRITING THE NOVEL FROM PLOT TO PRINT TO PIXEL • TELLING LIES FOR FUN & PROFIT • SPIDER, SPIN ME A WEB • WRITE FOR YOUR LIFE • THE LIAR'S BIBLE • THE LIAR'S COMPANION • AFTERTHOUGHTS

NON-FICTION

STEP BY STEP • GENERALLY SPEAKING • THE CRIME OF OUR LIVES • AFTERTHOUGHTS

ANTHOLOGIES EDITED

DEATH CRUISE • MASTER'S CHOICE • OPENING SHOTS • MASTER'S CHOICE 2 • SPEAKING OF LUST • OPENING SHOTS 2 • SPEAKING OF GREED • BLOOD ON THEIR HANDS • GANGSTERS, SWINDLERS, KILLERS, & THIEVES • MANHATTAN NOIR • MANHATTAN NOIR 2 • DARK CITY LIGHTS • IN SUNLIGHT OR IN SHADOW

WRITING AS JILL EMERSON

SHADOWS • WARM AND WILLING • ENOUGH OF SORROW • THIRTY • THREESOME • A MADWOMAN'S DIARY • THE TROUBLE WITH EDEN • A WEEK AS ANDREA BENSTOCK • GETTING OFF

THE CLASSIC CRIME LIBRARY

AFTER THE FIRST DEATH • DEADLY HONEYMOON • GRIFTER'S GAME • THE GIRL WITH THE LONG GREEN HEART • THE SPECIALISTS • THE TRIUMPH OF EVIL • SUCH MEN ARE DANGEROUS • NOT COMIN' HOME TO YOU • LUCKY AT CARDS • KILLING CASTRO • A DIET OF TREACLE • YOU COULD CALL IT MURDER • COWARD'S KISS • STRANGE EMBRACE • CINDERELLA SIMS • PASSPORT TO PERIL • ARIEL

THE COLLECTION OF CLASSIC EROTICA

21 GAY STREET • CANDY • GIGOLO JOHNNY WELLS • APRIL NORTH • CARLA • A STRANGE KIND OF LOVE • CAMPUS TRAMP

• COMMUNITY OF WOMEN • BORN TO BE BAD • COLLEGE FOR SINNERS • OF SHAME AND JOY • A WOMAN MUST LOVE • THE ADULTERERS • KEPT • THE TWISTED ONES • HIGH SCHOOL SEX CLUB • I SELL LOVE • 69 BARROW STREET • FOUR LIVES AT THE CROSSROADS • CIRCLE OF SINNERS • A GIRL CALLED HONEY • SIN HELLCAT • SO WILLING

THE MATTHEW SCUDDER NOVELS
THE SINS OF THE FATHERS • TIME TO MURDER AND CREATE • IN THE MIDST OF DEATH • A STAB IN THE DARK • EIGHT MILLION WAYS TO DIE • WHEN THE SACRED GINMILL CLOSES • OUT ON THE CUTTING EDGE • A TICKET TO THE BONEYARD • A DANCE AT THE SLAUGHTERHOUSE • A WALK AMONG THE TOMBSTONES • THE DEVIL KNOWS YOU'RE DEAD • A LONG LINE OF DEAD MEN • EVEN THE WICKED • EVERYBODY DIES • HOPE TO DIE • ALL THE FLOWERS ARE DYING • A DROP OF THE HARD STUFF • THE NIGHT AND THE MUSIC

THE BERNIE RHODENBARR MYSTERIES
BURGLARS CAN'T BE CHOOSERS • THE BURGLAR IN THE CLOSET • THE BURGLAR WHO LIKED TO QUOTE KIPLING • THE BURGLAR WHO STUDIED SPINOZA • THE BURGLAR WHO PAINTED LIKE MONDRIAN • THE BURGLAR WHO TRADED TED WILLIAMS • THE BURGLAR WHO THOUGHT HE WAS BOGART • THE BURGLAR IN THE LIBRARY • THE BURGLAR IN THE RYE • THE BURGLAR ON THE PROWL • THE BURGLAR WHO COUNTED THE SPOONS

KELLER'S GREATEST HITS
HIT MAN • HIT LIST • HIT PARADE • HIT & RUN • HIT ME • KELLER'S FEDORA

THE ADVENTURES OF EVAN TANNER
THE THIEF WHO COULDN'T SLEEP • THE CANCELED CZECH • TANNER'S TWELVE SWINGERS • TWO FOR TANNER • TANNER'S TIGER • TANNER'S VIRGIN • ME TANNER, YOU JANE • TANNER ON ICE

THE AFFAIRS OF CHIP HARRISON
NO SCORE • CHIP HARRISON SCORES AGAIN • MAKE OUT WITH MURDER • THE TOPLESS TULIP CAPER

WRITTEN FOR PERFORMANCE
TILT! (EPISODIC TELEVISION) • HOW FAR? (ONE-ACT PLAY) • MY BLUEBERRY NIGHTS (FILM)

Resume Speed
And Other Stories

LAWRENCE BLOCK

Publication History:
"Hard Sell", © 1960, *Ed McBain's Mystery Magazine*
"Dead to the World", © 1963, *Alfred Hitchcock's Mystery Magazine*
"Whatever It Takes", © 2016, *Alfred Hitchcock's Mystery Magazine*
"I Know How to Pick 'Em", © 2013, *Dangerous Women*
"Autumn at the Automat", © 2016, *In Sunlight or in Shadow*
"Gym Rat", © 2016, ePublished by *Crime Fiction Academy*
Resume Speed, © 2016, Subterranean Press

Cover and Interior: QA Productions

A LAWRENCE BLOCK PRODUCTION

Author's Foreword

Resume Speed.
And other stories.
You know, I get that far and suddenly I'm at a loss for words. On the one hand, I've said it all. On the other, well, what is there to say?

I've been trying to find a common element uniting the seven works of fiction in this book. There would seem to be three: I wrote them all, they're all comfortable under the broad canopy of crime fiction, and until now they haven't been collected. The earliest story was written in 1960, which is 58 years ago as I write these lines, and could slip even further into the past by the time you read them. Another came three years later. A third was written in the 1990s, lost for twenty years or more, and first published in 2016. The other four were written and published within the past several years.

So why don't I take them one at a time? A little trip down Memory Lane, undertaken while I still have some of my memory available to me, might be of some interest.

Hard Sell. Craig Rice was a very interesting woman, and an inventive and highly idiosyncratic writer. Her name at birth was Georgiana Ann Randolph Craig (although rumors advanced several other possible birth names for her, my own favorite of which was Craig Craig).

She was born in 1908 and died in 1957, and there's plenty more I could spoon-feed you, but in this miraculous era of Google and Wikipedia I'm happier letting you dig it out on your own.

I never met Craig, but she was represented by Scott Meredith while I was working there, and I heard stories about her and was close friends with the late Lawrence Janifer (then Larry M. Harris) who knew her and wrote a continuation of her John J. Malone series—*The Pickled Poodles*—after her death. (He got a byline on the book; earlier, when Craig wrote novels serialized in magazines, and failed to deliver the last chapter, he finished what she had started, but anonymously.)

Craig had a powerful thirst, which explains the undelivered final chapters and the short lifespan. After her death, Evan Hunter completed a book of which she had written about half, with no note to indicate where she planned to go with it. Evan thus had to solve the mystery in order to write it, and did so; the book, published as *The April Robin Murders*, bore the joint byline "by Craig Rice and Ed McBain."

Meanwhile, Larry Janifer went to work on *The Pickled Poodles*, published in 1960. And that was the same year that I was commissioned to write a John J. Malone short story, to be published in *Ed McBain's Mystery Magazine*. "Hard Sell" was the result. It appeared in the first issue of the magazine, and another story of mine, "Package Deal," was in the magazine's third issue. There was, alas, no fourth issue.

Years later, "Package Deal" found its way into a collection of my earliest crime stories, *One Night Stands and Lost Weekends*. I might have included "Hard Sell," but it was still known to be a Craig Rice story, and wound up in *Murder, Mystery and Malone*, edited by Jeffrey Marks and published in 2002 by Crippen & Landru. I let C&L know that I'd written "Hard Sell," and the word has been spread since then in various bibliographies. So, now that the cat is out of the clear plastic bag, it seems appropriate to tuck the story into a collection of my work.

*   *   *

Dead to the World. I was living in a suburb of Buffalo when I wrote this story. It owes existence to a fact I'd come across. That works very well at times; within a very short span of time I learned two interesting facts—that there were some individuals who did not sleep at all, perhaps because their hypothetical sleep center had been somehow rendered inoperative, and that there was still a Stuart pretender to the English throne. (The last reigning Stuart monarch was Anne, who died in 1714. The Jacobite cause essentially ended with the defeat of Bonnie Prince Charlie at Culloden in 1745. But, well, you never know.)

Those two facts would appear to have nothing much to do with one another, but my having happened on them at around the same time evidently had an effect. In time I came up with a fellow whose sleep center had been destroyed by North Korean shrapnel, and who spent his sleepless days and nights as a passionate devotee of lost causes, including that of the Stuart pretender. I named him Evan Tanner and wrote a book about him, *The Thief Who Couldn't Sleep*, and seven more books followed at irregular intervals.

Back to "Dead to the World." The idea that gave rise to it was the dangerous synergy of alcohol and sedative drugs. I wrote the story, a short-short, and by the time I'd finished it I'd decided that it wasn't much of an idea, and that I hadn't produced all that much of a story.

So I came up with another idea, this one for what you might call a marketing plan. I retyped the first page, changing the byline from *Lawrence Block* to *Sharon Wood Jeffries*, and sent it off to Henry Morrison, who was then working for Scott Meredith, of whose agency I was a client. (Some years earlier I'd been an employee myself, spending my days reading over-the-transom manuscripts, one worse than the next. I learned a great deal at that job. Some of what I learned was about the writing of fiction, while much was about the practice of chicanery.)

A few days later Henry called to say that he'd read the story, that he didn't think all that highly of it, and who the hell was Sharon Wood Jeffries?

"A schoolteacher," I said, "or possibly a librarian. She's never had anything published, so it's a perfect opportunity to submit it to *Ellery Queen's Mystery Magazine*. Their Department of First Stories might be receptive to a story that's a little weak—judging by some of the ones they've run."

Henry took a deep breath, and then another one. "No," he said. "We draw the line at that."

This was astonishing information, because I'd been under the impression that Scott Meredith didn't draw the line at anything. Henry said he'd try the story a couple of places, and we left it at that. The first place he tried it was *Alfred Hitchcock's Mystery Magazine*. *AHMM* and *EQMM* have been under a single roof since 1975, but back in the day *AHMM* was the creature of a company called HSD Publications, based in South Florida. Henry had sent them several stories of mine, and they bought them more often than not, and they bought this one. He may have told them it was my work, or he may not have bothered, even as he hadn't bothered to change the byline. At any rate it appeared in their issue for June, 1963, with Sharon's name on it—but they'd somehow excised her maiden name. She was now plain Sharon Jeffries.

And this was her first published story—and, sad to say, her last. By now I feel certain she's retired from that school or library. Perhaps she's living in Florida, not far from where they used to publish *AHMM* . . .

Never mind. I'd have collected "Dead to the World" before, as I could surely have found a place for it in *Enough Rope*, but I lost track of it entirely. Then I thought about it and asked about it, having remembered the byline even though I'd long since forgotten the title. Somebody sent me a photocopy, and I thought I ought to be able to do something with it, but that would require typing it up to get it in electronic form. So I put it in a box of stuff and forgot about it all over again.

Some hours ago, I came across it while I was going through that very box of stuff. "Oh, what the hell," I said, and sat down and typed it up.

And here it is.

Whatever It Takes. Here's another lost story, which I must have written in the late '80s or early '90s. It was certainly before I started using a computer, because I found a typescript of it in another box of stuff, along with a photocopy. That's what I would do then, type my work and get it copied before delivering the original to my agent. (Not too many years before that I'd have made a carbon copy. Do you remember carbon paper? Does anybody?)

If I'm going to lose a story, I generally wait until after it's published. But I lost "Whatever It Takes" before any editor got a chance to see it. Instead of taking it to my agent, or sending it somewhere on my own, I put it away—and completely forgot about it.

And then, twenty-plus years later, I was going through boxes of old manuscripts with an eye toward selling what I could to collectors. And there was my photocopy of "Whatever It Takes," and so was the original, typed on high-quality white bond paper.

I scanned the manuscript and sent the scan to Linda Landrigan at *AHMM*. She liked it, bought it, and found a home for it in the December 2016 issue.

Then I turned around and sold the manuscript to a collector.

*   *   *

I Know How to Pick 'Em was written for *Dangerous Women*, an original anthology edited by George R. R. Martin and Gardner Dozois. I'd have included it in my 2013 collection, *Catch and Release*, but the deal with the anthologists kept me from publishing it anywhere until a year after their book came out. I did ePublish it after an appropriate interval, and it got mostly nice reviews on Amazon, although I see now that a couple of readers absolutely hated it.

This was my second contribution to a Martin & Dozois collection. Earlier, for *Warriors*, I turned to Kit Tolliver, about whom I'd written three short stories; she'd already begun a career as a robber and serial murderer of her sexual partners, and in "Clean Slate" we get her backstory, and she gets her mission in life—to hunt down the five ex-lovers who'd escaped with their lives, and, um, kill them. By the time I finished "Clean Slate" I realized I was four chapters into a novel, and that I was crazy about Kit and wanted to tell her story in full.

The novel was *Getting Off*, and it was great fun to write. I rather doubt that there'll be more about the narrator-protagonist of "I Know How to Pick 'Em." But one never knows.

Autumn at the Automat. A couple of years ago I got a compelling idea from out of nowhere: an anthology of stories inspired by the paintings of Edward Hopper. I came up with a title, *In Sunlight or in Shadow*, cajoled a magnificent troupe of writers to pick paintings and write stories, and thought I really ought to pick a painting and write a story myself.

Hopper's work is wonderfully evocative. He's not a narrative painter, and his paintings don't tell stories. What they do, and more than any other artist I know, is suggest that there are stories to be told.

So I let Google Images show me more of his paintings than I'll ever have the chance to see on museum walls, and many of them spoke to me, but none of what they said seemed to me to be the stuff of fiction. Which is to say I didn't get any story ideas out of them.

And then, looking at *Automat*, I got a whole story in a rush. I knew exactly who that woman was, and what she was doing in that restaurant. That was the story I wanted to write, the story I *had* to write, and there was only one problem. Another writer, Kristine Kathryn Roush, had already selected *Automat*.

At the time, my wife and I were on an extended Holland America cruise of the North Atlantic. The ship had good Wi-Fi, and I emailed Kris, explained my situation, and asked her how far she'd gotten on the story. If she'd started writing, or if she had a compelling story idea, I'd find another painting. But if she was at all tentative about it—

She replied very graciously, saying she'd picked *Automat* because she'd had to make a selection, but she was by no means committed to it and could as easily choose something else. (And she did, turning in the magnificent "Still Life 1931," a powerful story of a civil rights activist years before the term existed.)

Meanwhile, I sat down in my cabin on the *Veendam* and wrote "Autumn at the Automat" in two days. That was in August of 2015, and sixteen months later Pegasus Books published *In Sunlight or in Shadow*, and in the months that followed my Automat story was nominated for just about everything short of a run for a Senate seat. Time after time I got to tell myself that having been nominated was honor enough, as that's what you're supposed to tell yourself when someone else wins, which is what kept happening. But in April 2017 I sat at the Pegasus table at Mystery Writers of America's annual awards dinner, and was gobsmacked when my story won an Edgar.

So here it is.

*   *   *

Gym Rat. Jonathan Santlofer, who somehow manages to operate with sheer virtuosity as both a writer and a fine artist, is also a good friend. Now and again he's written stories for my anthologies and I for his. He works closely with the Center for Fiction, an extraordinary resource in the process now of relocating from East 47th Street to downtown Brooklyn. But they hadn't yet begun the move when Jonathan invited me to participate in a project.

It had a couple of parts to it. First, I'd read two stories written by participants at the Crime Fiction Academy, a project of the Center for Fiction. I'd pick one of them. Then I'd write a story of my own, and it would be combined with the story I'd chosen in an ebook and published to Kindle. The Center for Fiction would get half the net income, which is nice, as they're a good cause. I'm a pretty good cause myself, and I'd get the other half.

I read the two Crime Fiction Academy finalists; both were excellent, but "The Murder Club" by Matt Plass was my choice. Then I forgot about it—do you notice a pattern here?—until Jonathan reminded me that the deadline was looming. I found myself thinking about some of the fellows I'd noticed at my gym, where I go as often as possible to raise and lower heavy objects to no apparent purpose.

And an idea for a story emerged. And I started writing, and the story took root and grew, until it came it at over 10,000 words. So I suppose it would be okay to call it not a story but a novelette. What I called it was "Gym Rat." In tandem with "The Murder Club," it was Kindle-published in December of 2016. And every now and then I get a check, which is always nice.

I probably could have sent it to a magazine, but, well, I never got around to it, so its sole existence has been electronic. How nice to be able to tuck it into a book!

*   *   *

Resume Speed. I see I've nattered on a bit about the way ideas for stories are generated and develop. And that serves as a good lead-in to this volume's title story. I know exactly when the germ of the idea was planted.

Well, almost exactly. 1978, I think, but I could be off by a year. It would have been a Sunday night, though, because there was a group that met on Sunday nights, and it was at one of their meetings a fellow told his story, of which I remember almost nothing.

Nothing but this: He had for years led a peripatetic life, moving frequently from one locale to another. And one morning he awoke with no memory whatsoever of the last few hours of the previous evening.

This was not unusual. He was a heavy drinker seven days a week, and blackouts were a frequent result. But this was different, because he woke up convinced he must have done something horrible. He'd never in his life done anything significantly bad, and yet on this occasion he was consumed with dread. Surely he'd transgressed in a major way, surely he'd said something irretrievably nasty, surely he'd disgraced himself in ways he could not even imagine. And, since he had not memory of where he'd been or in what company, he didn't have a clue as to whom he owed an apology, or for what.

So he packed his suitcase and left town. He'd been employed at the time, but his boss never saw him again. Neither did his circle of friends. He was outta there, and he never looked back.

I loved the story, though it didn't occur to me to do anything with it.

Until 38 years later, when I was on an Amtrak train returning from Bouchercon, a sort of floating crap game for mystery writers and readers, held in a different city every year. (Not, I should stress, because the conference disgraces itself, although some of the participating writers very well may. It moves on because anyone who hosts the conference needs years to recover from the experience.)

This was October of 2015, and the host city was Raleigh, a burg well worth a visit for the Laotian restaurant alone. I was traveling alone, and for God knows what reason I thought about Mack, who'd told that story all those years ago. (That was his first name, Mack. He was a tall man, and a beefy one. And that, alas, is absolutely all I know about the fellow—beside the fact that he woke up from a blackout and hightailed it out of town.)

There's a story there, I thought for the very first time. I came home, and before very long I started writing it. Initially I'd been thinking in terms of a simple short story, perhaps 3–4000 words long, but I got into the story and into the character, all the characters, and I let the story tell me how long it wanted to be. It wound up running a little over 20,000 words.

Amazon took it for a Kindle Single, in which capacity it's done quite nicely over the years. And Bill Schafer of Subterranean Press loved *Resume Speed* and published it in hardcover, in both a signed limited and a trade edition. Both are out of print.

Another novella, *Keller's Fedora*, had a similar history, and after a few years it occurred to me that it might work as a paperback. I self-published it in that form, and it's regularly my top-selling paperback. Could I do the same with this novella?

Well, I could do it, but I might have a tough time getting people to buy it. The Keller novella was longer by several thousand words, and had the commercial advantage of being about a popular character. Hmmm. Maybe if I found some other hitherto uncollected stories to fill out the volume . . .

And this book you are clutching, Gentle Reader, is the result. Seven tales, running to just under 50,000 words—surely a respectable length for a paperback book.

Not to mention that this introduction of mine has somehow added another 3300 words to the count . . .

Hard Sell

"Malone," the voice said, "you've got to help me."

The little lawyer waggled a finger at Joe the Angel and sat impassive while the bartender poured another double shot of rye. Then he swallowed the rye, reflecting thoughtfully that clients were always turning up when you needed them the least. "I don't have to help you," he said without bothering to turn around. "My office rent is paid a month in advance. My secretary is paid a week in advance. My bar tab is paid several drinks in advance. So go away."

"Money," said the voice, "is no object."

"That's what I've been trying to tell you," Malone said. "Besides, if you want me, why don't you call me at my office?"

"I tried," the voice admitted. "I talked to a girl named Maggie. She said *this* was your office."

Malone turned around, deciding firmly that Maggie would never again be paid anything in advance. He found himself looking at a large man with iron-gray hair, blue eyes, and a prominent chin. The man looked so healthy that Malone wanted to turn away again. "Go ahead," he said. "Tell me about it."

"Can't we go someplace private?"

"This is my office," Malone reminded him. "How private can you get?"

The man looked around vacantly, then back at Malone. "My name is Gunderson," he said. "Frank Gunderson. Mean anything to you?"

"Nothing," Malone said. "So far."

"I sell magazine subscriptions," Gunderson announced.

"That's nice," Malone said pleasantly. "Working your way through college?"

Gunderson looked very unhappy. "I don't exactly sell them," he explained. "I employ salesmen. Gunderson Sales, Inc. Door-to-door sales of leading magazines. A customer buys one or two magazines and gets another free. It's a very attractive offer."

"I'm sure it is," the little lawyer agreed. "But I can't read. So you're wasting my time."

"You don't understand," Gunderson said. "It's like this, Malone. Somebody's been killing my salesmen. One after the other, day after day, my men have been murdered."

"By prospective customers?"

"By a fiend," Gunderson said. "First Joe Tallmer, struck down brutally by a hit-and-run driver. That was a week ago. Then, two days later, Leon Prince was pushed into an empty elevator shaft. The very next day, somebody shoved Howie Kirshmeyer from an elevated platform and an oncoming train mangled him. And—"

Malone help up a hand, both to silence Gunderson and to summon Joe the Angel. He downed the double rye that Joe poured and fixed sad eyes on Gunderson.

"Accidents," he said soberly, "can happen."

"But, Malone—"

"Three accidents," he went on. "The first one got hit by a car. The second one was too dumb to wait for the elevator. The third one tried to walk across the tracks. It figures, in a way. Anyone dumb enough to sell magazines for a living—"

"You don't understand," Gunderson cut in. "There was a fourth one. Just this morning."

"What happened to him?"

"He was shot through the head with a .45," Gunderson said. "He's dead," he added unnecessarily.

John J. Malone suddenly felt very tired. "Sounds like murder," he admitted, "but I'm sure the police can take care of it."

"I don't see how," Gunderson said. "The man's name was Henry Littleton. He was sitting over coffee while his wife was upstairs making the beds or something. Somebody came in, shot him, and left."

"The gun?"

"It was on the breakfast-room table. No prints, no registration."

"Hmmmm," Malone said.

"You see," Gunderson continued, "the police can do nothing. Littleton wasn't murdered by someone who knew him. He was murdered for the same reason as Tallmer and Prince and Kirschmeyer."

"And why were *they* murdered?"

"I wish I knew," Gunderson said. "I wish I knew."

Malone paused to light a cigar. "Come, now," he said gently. "You must have some idea. Otherwise you wouldn't be here annoying me."

Gunderson hesitated. "Malone," he said, "I don't want to sound paranoid. But I think someone is trying to ruin me, Malone. Killing my men one after the other. Crippling my sales force. Two of my men quit me today, Malone. Left me cold. Told me they couldn't take the chance of working for me. One of 'em said he had a wife and kid. Hell, *I've* got a wife and kid. Two kids, as a matter of fact. And—"

"Shut up for a minute," the little lawyer said absently. "Who would want to cripple your sales force? You have any competition in this little con game of yours?"

Gunderson colored. "It's not a con game. But I do have a competitor."

"Does he have a name?"

"Tru-Val Subscriptions," Gunderson said.

Malone sighed. "That's a strange name for a man," he remarked. "What do they call him for short? Troovie?"

"That's the company name, Malone. The man's name is Harold Cowperthwaite."

Malone looked around vacantly. He could understand the murder of door-to-door salesmen, especially if such murder were performed by dissident customers. But he didn't *want* to understand, not now. He didn't want the case at all.

"Malone? Here's a check. Twenty-five hundred dollars. I'll have another check for twenty-five hundred for you when you clear this up. Plus expenses, of course. Will that be sufficient?"

Malone took the check and found a place for it in his wallet. He nodded pleasantly at Gunderson and watched the man leave the City Hall Bar, walking with a firm stride, arms swinging, chest out. Then he looked around until he found Joe the Angel again and pointed to his empty glass. It was, he decided, time to begin piling up expenses for Gunderson.

Harold Cowperthwaite was not helpful. He looked as sickly as Gunderson looked vigorous, and was just about as much fun to be with. Malone decided that he disliked them both equally.

"—incredible accusation!" Cowperthwaite had just finished shouting. "A couple of his doorbell punchers keel over and he blames me for it! Blames me for everything! Ought to sue him for libel! Serve him right!"

Malone sighed, wishing the little man wouldn't talk exclusively in exclamation points. "Then you didn't kill them," he suggested.

"Kill them!" boomed Cowperthwaite. "Course I didn't kill them!

I wanted to kill anybody I'd kill Gunderson! Know what I think, Malone?"

Malone was totally unprepared for the question mark. "Hmmm," he said, "what *do* you think?"

"Think he killed 'em himself!" Cowperthwaite shouted. "Throw suspicion on me! Make trouble for me! People bothering me all the time!"

"Oh," said Malone. "No, he couldn't have done that."

"No?"

"Of course not," Malone said. "He's my client."

Cowperthwaite's words followed the lawyer out of the door marked *Tru-Val Subscriptions.* Malone managed to close the door before the man reached the last exclamation point. It was, he decided, a day for small triumphs.

"The way I see it," von Flanagan said, "we wait until he kills another one. Then maybe he leaves a clue."

"He?" Malone said, lost. "Who he?"

"The killer," the big cop said. "The bird who killed Littleton and the others without leaving a trace. Pretty soon he'll find another magazine salesman and kill him. Maybe we get lucky and catch him in the act. Wouldn't that be nice?"

"For everybody but the magazine salesman," Malone agreed. "You don't seem to be taking much of an interest in this one. Something wrong?"

"Plenty," von Flanagan said. "For one thing, it's an impossible one to solve. For another, I don't want to solve it."

"Why not?"

Von Flanagan shook his head wearily. "Malone?" he said. "Have you ever had a run-in with a magazine salesman? Have you ever had one of those little monsters stick his foot in your door and tell you how much you needed his rotten magazines? Have you, Malone?"

Malone nodded.

"They should kill every last one of them," von Flanagan said. "I mean it, Malone. Anybody kills a magazine salesman he deserves a medal."

Malone sighed. "The case," he reminded von Flanagan. "Let's talk about the case. Tell me all about it. Everything."

"There's not much to tell," von Flanagan said, relaxing into a chair. "This Littleton is thirty-three years old, has a wife and two kids. One is a boy and the other—"

"—is a girl," Malone guessed.

"You know the story? Then why bother me?"

"I'm sorry," Malone said. "Please go on."

"He's a hustler," said von Flanagan. "Holds down two jobs at once. Works real hard. Sells magazines evenings for this Gunderson character and works nine to five in a garage. Hasn't got any money, though. He's had a tough run of luck lately. Doctor bills, things going wrong with the kids, you know. But he's not in debt either. A good, steady guy. A guy you might like if he wasn't a magazine salesman."

"The crime," Malone said gently.

"Murder," von Flanagan said. "Not by the wife, either. I thought of that, Malone. I didn't want to because she's such a sweet little woman. A doll. But she was upstairs with the kids at the time. The kids said so. They wouldn't lie. Too young to lie."

Malone lit a cigar. "He was shot by somebody inside the house?"

Von Flanagan nodded. "At close range," he said. "It almost looked as though the killer wanted to make it look like suicide. But he didn't try very hard. No powder burns, for one thing, and the gun was lying near Littleton's left hand. And he was right-handed. We checked."

"Clever of you," the lawyer said. "So it was murder, and not by the wife. How about the other salesmen? Tallmer and Prince and Kirkenberger?"

"Kirschmeyer," von Flanagan corrected. "That's the funny part of it. Tallmer was a typical hit-and-run. Prince and Kirschmeyer look more like accidents than most accidents. But with them all coming together like this—"

"I know," Malone said gloomily. "Did Littleton have any insurance?"

"Insurance?" von Flanagan looked lost. "Oh," he said. "Littleton, insurance. Yeah. A big policy. But that's out, Malone. The wife is the only beneficiary and she's clear. So that's out."

"Thanks," Malone said. "So am I."

"So are you what?"

"Out," Malone said. "For a drink."

With two double ryes under his belt and a pair of beer chasers keeping them company, Malone felt in condition to use the phone. He called Charlie Stein, a useful little man who served as Dun and Bradstreet for a world far removed from Wall Street, running credit checks for gamblers and similarly unsavory elements.

"Take your time on this one," he told Stein. "Nothing urgent. I want to find out if there's anything around on a man named Henry Littleton. And," he added sadly, "there probably isn't."

"You're wrong," Stein said. "There is."

Malone came back to life. "Go on," he said. "Talk to me."

"Henry Littleton," Stein said. "He's into Max Hook for seventy-five grand. That all you want to know?"

"That's impossible," Malone said. "I mean—"

"Impossible but true."

"Oh," Malone said. "Well, you better cross him off, Charlie. Somebody shot him in the head."

Malone hung up quickly, then lifted the receiver again and put through a call to Max Hook. The gambler picked up the phone almost at once. "Malone, Max," Malone said cheerfully. "You didn't order a hit for a guy named Henry Littleton, did you?"

"Littleton? That's the fink who owes me seventy-five grand. Seventy-five *grand* he owes me and a nickel at a time he pays me. That guy." There was a pause. Then, with the air of someone just now hearing what Malone said in the first place, Hook said, "You saying somebody chilled him?"

"This morning. It wasn't you, was it?"

"Of course not," Hook said. "Why kill somebody who owes me money? That doesn't make sense, Malone."

"I didn't think it did," Malone said pleasantly. "Just checking, Max." He put the receiver on the hook and made his way back to the bar.

"You don't look so hot," Joe the Angel said thoughtfully. "You want me to leave the bottle?"

Malone sighed. "Don't be ridiculous," he said. "Then I wouldn't have anybody to talk to." He closed his eyes and tried to think. This Littleton had been hard-working, honest, and seventy-five thousand dollars in debt. Hook hadn't killed him, and Cowperthwaite hadn't killed him, and his wife hadn't killed him, and he hadn't committed suicide. The whole thing was terrifying.

"I'm glad I found you," von Flanagan was saying. "You're drunk, but I'm still glad I found you. I want to tell you you've been wasting your time. We thought there was a connection between the salesmen. But there isn't."

"You're wrong," Malone said magnificently. "But go on anyway."

"Tallmer," von Flanagan said, ignoring the interruption. "The first one. A guy walked into the station-house and said he was the hitter-and-runner. Conscience was bothering him. And there was no connection between him and the rest. Accidents. Like we figured."

"Wrong," said Malone sadly. "Completely wrong."

"Huh?"

"I'll explain," said Malone. "I will tell all. I sort of thought something like this would happen." He sighed. "Tallmer was a typical hit-and-run. That much you know."

"That much I told you."

Malone nodded. "Prince and Kirschenblum—"

"Kirschmeyer."

"To hell with it," said Malone. "Anyway, the two of them were murdered. By the same person who killed Littleton."

"If you're so smart," said von Flanagan, "then you can tell me that person's name. The one who killed them all."

"Simple," said Malone. "The name is Littleton."

He explained while von Flanagan sat there gaping. "Littleton was in debt," he said. "Seventy-five grand in debt. With no way out. Then Tallmer got hit by car."

"Precisely," said von Flanagan.

"And Littleton got an idea," he said. "He wanted to kill himself but he didn't want his wife to lose the insurance. So he killed himself and made it look like murder."

Malone lit a fresh cigar. "He set up a chain," he went on. "Chucked Prince down an elevator shaft and heaved Kirschengruber in front of the elevated."

"Kirschmeyer."

"You know who I mean. Anyway, Littleton did this, and set up a chain. A subtle chain. Then he shot himself."

"Left-handed? From a distance?"

"Of course," Malone said. "If you wanted to make it look like a murder, would you use your right hand and put the gun in your mouth? See?"

Von Flanagan thought it over. "So it's suicide," he said. "And we write it off as murder and suicide, with Littleton the murderer. Right?"

"Wrong," Malone said. "You write Prince and Kicklebutton off as accidents and Littleton as murder by person or persons unknown. If he went to all that trouble there's no sense in conning the wife and kids out of the insurance. Besides, you'd never get a suicide verdict. Not unless I persuaded the coroner's inquest. And I won't."

Von Flanagan shrugged. "How are you going to collect your fee?"

"I'll tell Gunderson his salesmen are safe," Malone said. "I'll offer to repay the fee in full if another one gets murdered. And if that's not enough for him, he can keep the twenty-five hundred he owes me. Remember, I didn't want this case in the first place."

Dead to the World

Ellen drove home from the Spragues' house. Roy had first attempted to do the driving himself, but he let himself be talked out of it; he had a tendency to wrap his car around a tree after parties. So Ellen drove, and he sprawled upon the seat beside her, his head tossed back at an awkward angle.

It had been a usual sort of party, with Roy cast as the life of it. He told all the jokes, kissed all the women, and drank almost all of the Scotch. All of the men laughed loudly at his jokes and said what a great fellow he was, telling themselves all the while that they were damned glad they didn't drink the way Roy Farrell did. The women flirted with Roy and pitied Ellen with their eyes, thanking the stars for their own husbands all the while. Throughout the evening, Ellen played the role of the wife who loved her husband dearly in spite of his faults, faults which became progressively more obvious as the night moved onward.

Roy Farrell was the third husband whom she had loved in spite of his faults. Ellen seemed to be accident-prone in a very special way. She kept marrying alcoholics. She had married Fred Land first, had lived with him for five intoxicating years, during which all her friends wondered to themselves and to one another how she could possibly stand it. He died, and she married Arnold Beadle, and Arnold Beadle drank twice as much as Fred ever drank. For three more years her friends wondered how she stood him, until he dropped dead after an especially exuberant debauch.

Now she was married to Roy Farrell, a florid-faced red-eyed man who made both her late husbands look like teetotalers, and by now her friends had given up wondering. Evidently Ellen had a compulsion about alcoholics; she married them as other women adopted stray cats.

Odd, too, because Ellen herself never touched a drop. She never lectured her husbands, never dragged them bodily to temperance meetings, never opened precious bottles to pour their contents down the drain. She merely endured.

"Fine wife for any man," Roy said suddenly. He sat up and peered around vacantly. "My girl," he said.

"Try to rest, dear."

"Ummm," Roy said thoughtfully. He closed his eyes and passed out again.

Ellen drove her car into the driveway, opened her door, and walked around the car to open the door on Roy's side. It took her a moment to get him on his feet. He finally draped a limp arm around her neck and let her guide him into the house. She eased him into an armchair and went around the living room putting on lights.

"Don't feel good," Roy Farrell said.

"We'd better get to bed, dear."

"Want a drink," Roy Farrell said.

"And then will you go to bed?"

"Ummm," he said.

She found an open bottle of Scotch in the dining room cabinet and poured him a double shot. She started toward the living room, then stopped, set the glass down, and went to the medicine chest. When she came back with the glass of liquor in one hand and a pill in the other he was staring ahead blindly, his jaws slack.

"I think you ought to take a sedative tonight," she said.

He took the pill from her, examined it. He said, "What is it?"

"Just phenobarbital, dear."

"Stuff you take?"

"That's right."

" 'Cause you're nervous is why you got to take it. I make you nervous, Ellie?"

"Don't worry about me," she said. "Take your pill and drink your drink. You'll get a good might's sleep for a change."

"Ummm," he said. He took his pill and drank his drink. She took a phenobarbital tablet for herself and washed it down with two tall glasses of tap water. Then she helped Roy into the bedroom, undressed him, got him into bed. She hung his clothes neatly in his closet. By the time she lay in bed at his side, he was already snoring lightly. She closed her eyes and let the sedative take hold of her and whisk her off to sleep.

In the morning when Ellen awoke she lay still for several minutes with her face pressed to her pillow. The room was very silent. She listened for ragged breathing or heavy snoring and heard neither. Some mornings a bad hangover woke Roy early, sent him stumbling out of the house or kept him noisily ill in the bathroom. She yawned luxuriously, then rolled over onto her side.

Roy was there, sprawled on his back, his hands at his sides, his mouth open, his eyes shut. He looked infinitely peaceful. She smiled at him, then continued to stare at him while her smile faded and died. She put a hand over her own heart and felt it pounding furiously. She reached to touch Roy. He did not seem to be breathing.

She grabbed his wrist, felt for a pulse. There was none. She crouched over him and pressed an ear against his bare chest; she could not hear his heart beating.

Ellen forced herself to sit back, tried to make her own heart slow down by pure force of will. It hammered madly. With one hand still pressed to her chest, she turned in the bed and reached slowly for the telephone.

The doctor had a long face and sad eyes. He stirred the cup of coffee Ellen had made for him but did not drink it. Ellen sat across the breakfast table. She was calm now, he had given her a shot of something, and her nerves had ceased to be a problem.

"He was perfectly all right last night," she said her voice oddly steady. "When I woke up, I thought he was sleeping, but he was—"

The doctor nodded gently. "Unusual," he said. "But men who drink the way Roy Farrell drank, they kill themselves by inches. The human body is a wonderful machine. It can take all kinds of punishment. But like any machine, sooner or later it breaks down." He shook his head. "Heart failure, I'm afraid. It couldn't have been hard for him. He simply died in his sleep."

Ellen shivered.

"And yet it's surprising," the doctor continued. "I saw Roy just two months ago, gave him a complete physical, EKG and all. I told him he could look forward to liver trouble within the next five years if he didn't cut back on his drinking. But his heart was sound. Of course you can never tell with an alcoholic. They do horrible things to their bodies. Roy's heart, though—I never expected trouble from that area just now."

Ellen said nothing. The doctor stirred his coffee, raised the cup to his lips. Then he put it down abruptly.

"Would you object to an autopsy?"

"Why? Is it—"

"Necessary? I don't suppose so. I'm curious, though. I wouldn't order an autopsy against your wishes, Ellen, but—"

He let the sentence trail off. She looked at him vacantly. "If you think it's important," she said.

"It might be." He actually sipped the coffee this time. "Roy had a lot to drink last night, didn't he?"

"We were at a party. Ken and Mary Sprague."

"That answers that question. Did he exert himself especially? Take any drugs, stuff himself with food? Sit in the car with the motor running? Anything?"

Her eyes narrowed. "No," she said finally. "We came home, he had one drink before bed, I made him take something to help him sleep—"

"What?"

"Phenobarbital," she said. "I take it myself quite frequently, it's just a mild . . . Is something wrong?"

"Drugs," the doctor said heavily.

"I don't—"

"People should be told these things," the doctor said. "A drug that's perfectly safe in one instance is dynamite in combination with other ingredients. Phenobarb's a perfect example. Mild, safe, effective—unless you've got a load of alcohol in your bloodstream. Then it can easily be fatal."

"Oh, my God!"

"Ellen—"

"I made him take it," she said. "I thought it would help him relax, and I wanted him to get a good night's sleep. I made him take it!"

He took her hand.

"I killed Roy," she said.

"Easy now," he said. It took him a few moments to calm her down. "You couldn't know," he kept saying. "People don't know these things. They should, but they don't. Some people take nitroglycerine for angina. With a certain body chemistry, alcohol and nitroglycerine can combine to produce a type of temporary insanity, a very violent form.

There are dozens of combinations like that. You couldn't be expected to know, Ellen. You did nothing wrong!"

She was crying.

"And he'd have drunk himself to death soon enough anyway. Don't blame yourself, Ellen."

"I was just trying to help him," she said.

"I know."

After the doctor left she spent a long time sitting in her chair and gazing off into space. The future yawned before her. Roy's funeral, a black dress neatly accenting her graveside pallor, her hands locked together, her mouth quite grim. She would have to endure their pity. *Poor Ellen, all alone, but she's better of this way, better without him than with him.*

She would mourn Roy, and then she would live her life alone, and then she would marry again. She knew in advance the sort of man she would pick. Another of the hollow ones, another of the sort that measure out their live in shot glasses. She would marry such a man, and her friends would shake their heads and begin to pity her once again.

She would care for that new husband. She would fetch him bottles when his supply ran out. She would laugh at his jokes, she would hold his hand, she would drive home from parties and tuck him tenderly into bed. And she would see that he never, never, never took phenobarbital.

Something else would do as well.

Whatever It Takes

"Testify against Ben Billig," the fat man said. "You gotta be kidding, asking me to do that."

"Your testimony could put him away," Dattner said.

"Ha," the fat man said. "Put me away is more like it. Why don't you make it easy on me? Why don't you say, 'Cooperman, we got a favor we want you to do for us, would you please go and drink a can of Drano.' Then I can just drink it an' roll around on the floor an' die, save us all a lot of aggravation."

"We can relocate you, Mel."

"Billing can relocate me," Cooperman said. "Look at all the guys he relocated over the years. This one under the Jersey Turnpike, this one under the Garden State. Planted a couple in the Meadowlands, every time Lawrence Taylor sacks the quarterback he's running over a couple of unmarked graves. I don't want nobody to relocate me, thanks just the same. I like my present location just fine."

"We can give you a new name and a new face, Mel," Keith Harling said. "You know how the program works."

" 'Deed I do. You give me a new face and Ben Billig sends somebody to rip it off. What I'll do, I'll keep the one I got. It's not pretty but I'm used to it, you know what I mean?"

*   *   *

"If we could get him to testify," Harling said, "we could put Ben Billig away for some three or four consecutive life sentences. But he won't do it."

"He's got to," Dattner said. "What does he want? There's got to be something he wants. Whatever it is, let's give it to him. I'll do whatever it takes to nail Billig."

"What do I want?" Cooperman thought about it. "I want lots of things. I want to be able to eat whatever I want, never gain an ounce. You figure you can help me with that one?"

"What else do you want?"

"Oh, the usual. World peace, cure for cancer. You know what else'd be nice? A special mute button on the remote control for the TV, you use it for Monday Night Football, it shuts up the announcers but you still hear the crowd noise. You got your lab guys working on something like that?"

"Seriously, Mel."

"Seriously, quit wasting everybody's time. You can't give me nothing's gonna make up for what Billig'd give me. You give me a Rolls-Royce, how's I gonna drive it with my throat cut? If I talk I'm dead."

"If you don't talk you're going to jail."

"So? They feed you, they give you a bed to sleep in, even teach you a trade. Beats dying."

"Here's the problem," Harling said. "He's more afraid of Billig than he is of us. And can you blame him?"

"I've got an idea," Dattner said.

*   *   *

"Very decent of you," Cooperman said. "If I don't agree to testify, you'll put the word on the street, let everybody know I *did* agree to testify. Say I call your bluff. What good's it do you? He kills me, how can I testify for you? I think you're bluffing."

"Can you afford to call?"

"Gimme a phone." He lifted the receiver, dialed. "It's Mel. Can I talk to Ben, please? Ben, it's Mel. Couple of feds are trying to hammer me, say they'll put the word out I'm gonna rat you out. Case you hear it, remember I told you in front it was crap." He hung up, smiled at the two men. "So? You want, put the word out. If you don't, you'll be making me look like a liar."

"We may have made a mistake," Harling said. "He was real cute on the phone, but Billig might decide not to take any chances. He could take Mel Cooperman out just to play it safe."

"I don't care about Cooperman," Dattner said.

"He's a human being."

"He's pond scum," Dattner said. "But Billig is liver cancer. He's the kind of guy who gives criminal psychopaths a bad name. I don't care if I put Mel Cooperman under the gun. I'd do anything to get Billig."

"If only there was something to do."

"I've got an idea," Dattner said.

"I don't get it," Cooperman said. "Don't you guys ever give up? Didn't I tell you what I told you?"

"What happened to your windows?"

"Over there? The glass was old. I figured let's do it right, replace it all in one shot."

"I understand someone drove by and shot up the front of your house."

"You heard that, huh?"

"Billig just tried to kill you, you damned fool. Why not put him away before he does the job right?"

Cooperman shook his head. "If somebody shot up my living room windows," he said, "that don't mean anybody was trying to kill me. That's what you call a warning. That's just Ben making sure it don't slip my mind that I got no cause to testify against him. So I got to replace a little broken glass, putty up a few bullet holes in the far wall. You think that's so terrible? I don't think that's so terrible."

"You said something the other day about having an idea," Harling said. "Whatever it is, you'd better not wait too long. The other day some of Billig's goons shot out Cooperman's living room windows."

"I heard about that."

"And this morning," Harling said, "Cooperman found a bomb under the hood of his car."

"Some bomb," Cooperman said. "A clock and some wires and two sticks of dynamite. What do you need a clock for if you're wiring the thing to the ignition? And nothing was hooked up right, and there was no cap to set the dynamite off. It was another warning, that's all."

"If he trusts you," Dattner said, "why would he keep warning you? One of these times he's going to take you out."

Cooperman shook his head. "He's got no cause," he said, "and he knows that. I'm not worried."

That was the trouble, Dattner thought. The son of a bitch remained unworried. He'd done what he could to scare him, shooting up the front of his house, then attaching the fake bomb beneath the hood of his car. Of course he hadn't wired the bomb correctly. With his luck Cooperman would have neglected to check under the hood, and the bomb would have wiped out the best hope they had for putting Ben Billig where he unquestionably belonged.

A near miss was no good. A near miss would just be written off as a warning. The only way to scare Cooperman, the only way to make him believe Billig was trying to kill him, was to wing the bastard.

Cooperman was in his backyard now, grilling steaks on a charcoal fire. Dattner, perched on the back porch of a vacant house two hundred yards away, studied the fat man through the scope sight of a Czech-made rifle. One in the arm, he decided, but which arm? Cooperman seemed to be righthanded, he held the barbeque fork in his right hand. No sense incapacitating him any more than necessary, he thought, and he centered the crosshairs on Cooperman's fleshy upper arm.

Just as his finger settled on the trigger, the man moved. Dattner made a face and took careful aim again. He braced himself against the rifle's recoil and squeezed the trigger.

The bullet was wide to Cooperman's right. The report of the rifle reached him and he spun around wildly, trying to determine where the shot had come from. Dattner tried to center the gun's sights upon the now-moving target. He squeezed off a shot and missed again, and Cooperman dropped to the ground and rolled himself in a ball, artfully presenting no inconsequential portions of his anatomy to

Dattner. Through the telescope sight all Dattner could see was the back of Cooperman's head and the slope of his upper back.

"Oh, hell," Dattner said. He aimed right into the middle of Cooperman, set himself, and kept squeezing the trigger until the clip was empty.

"He'll never testify now," Harling said. "But don't let it get you. He wasn't going to anyway. And now Billig has sealed his lips forever."

"Maybe we can get the shooter," Dattner suggested, "and link him to Billig."

"No point even trying." He laid a hand on Dattner's shoulder. "I know how much this one meant to you," he said. "But sometimes there's nothing you can do. Billig's the kind of man who never leaves you an opening. As scared as Cooperman was of him, Billig had him taken out anyway. There's nothing we can do."

Dattner went home and cleaned his rifle. He remembered how the gun had felt in his hands, how all his anger and all his determination had sent those bullets ripping into Mel Cooperman. But it hadn't been Cooperman he'd been angry at.

He thought, *Nothing we can do? Nothing?*

He loaded a fresh clip into the rifle and carried it out to his car.

I Know How to Pick 'Em

I sure know how to pick 'em.

Except I don't know as I've got any credit coming for this one, because it's hard to make the case that it was me that picked her. She walked into that edge-of-town roadhouse with the script all worked out in her mind, and all that was left to do was cast the lead.

The male lead, that is. Far as the true leading role was concerned, well, that belonged to her. That much went without saying. Woman like her, she'd have to be the star in all of her productions.

They had a juke box, of course. Loud one. Be nice if I recalled what was playing when she crossed the threshold, but I wasn't paying attention—to the music, or to who came through the door. I had a beer in front of me, surprise surprise, and I was looking into it like any minute now it would tell me a secret.

Yeah, right. All any beer ever said to me was *Drink me down, horse. I might make things better and I sure can't make 'em worse.*

It was a country juke box, which you could have guessed from the parking lot, where the pickups outnumbered the Harleys by four or five to one. So if I can't say what was playing when she came in, or even when I looked up from my PBR and got a look at her, I can tell you what wasn't playing. "I Only Have Eyes For You."

That wasn't coming out of that juke box. But it should have been.

She was the beauty. Her face was all high cheekbones and sharp angles, and a girl who was just plain pretty would get all washed out standing next to her. She wasn't pretty herself, and a quick first glance might lead you to think that she wasn't attractive at all, but you'd look again and that first thought would get so far lost you'd forget you ever had it. There are fashion models with that kind of face. Film actresses, too, and they're the ones who keep on getting the good parts in their forties and fifties, when the pretty girls start looking like soccer moms and nosy neighbors.

And she only had eyes for me. Large well-spaced eyes, a rich brown in color, and I swear I felt them on me before I was otherwise aware of her presence. Looked up, caught her looking at me, and she saw me looking and didn't look away.

I suppose I was lost right there.

She was a blonde, with her hair cut to frame and flatter her face. She was tall, say five-ten, five-eleven. Slender but curvy. Her blouse was silk, with a bold geometric print. It was buttoned too high to show a lot of cleavage, but when she moved it would cling to her and let you know what it wasn't showing.

The way her jeans fit, well, you all at once understood why people paid big money for designer jeans.

The joint wasn't crowded, it was early, but there were people between her and me. She flowed through them and they melted away. The bartender, a hard-faced old girl with snake tattoos, came over to take a drink order.

The blonde had to think it over. "I don't know," she said to me. "What should I have?"

"Whatever you want."

She put her hand on my arm. I was wearing a long-sleeved shirt, so her skin and mine never touched, but they might as well.

"Pick a drink for me," she said.

I was looking down at her hand, resting there on my forearm. Her fingernails were medium-long, their polish the bright color of arterial bleeding.

Pick a drink for her? The ones that came quickest to mind were too fancy for the surroundings. Be insulting to order her a shot and a beer. Had to be a cocktail, but one that the snake lady would know how to make.

I said, "Lady'll have a Cuervo margarita." Her hand was on my right arm, so rather than move it I used my left hand to poke the change I'd left on the bar top, indicating that the margarita was on me.

"And the same for you? Or another Blue Ribbon?"

I shook my head. "But you could give me a Joey C. twice to keep it company."

"Thank you," my blonde said, while the bartender went to work. "That's a perfect choice, a margarita."

The drinks came, hers in a glass with a salted rim, my double Cuervo in an oversize shot glass. She let go of my arm and picked up her drink, raised the glass in a wordless toast. I left my Cuervo where it was and returned the toast with my beer.

She didn't throw her drink back like a sailor, but didn't take a little Baby Bird sip, either. She drank some and put the glass on the bar and her hand on my arm.

Nice.

No wedding ring. I'd noticed that right away, and hadn't needed a second glance to see that there'd been a ring on that finger, that it had come off recently enough to show not only the untanned band where the ring had been but the depression it had caused in the flesh. It said a lot, that finger. That she was married, and that she'd deliberately taken off her ring before entering the bar.

Hey, didn't I say? I know how to pick 'em.

*   *   *

But didn't I also say she picked me?

And picked that lowdown roadhouse for the same reason. If my type was what she was looking for, that was the place to find it.

My type: Well, big. Built like a middle linebacker, or maybe a tight end. Six-five, 230, big in the shoulders, narrow in the waist. More muscles than a man needs, unless he's planning to lift a car out of a rut.

Which I don't make a habit of. Not that good at lifting my poor self out of a rut, let alone an automobile.

Clean-shaven, when I shave; I was a day away from a razor when she came in and put her hand on my arm. But no beard, no mustache. Hair's dark and straight, and I haven't lost any of it yet. But I haven't hit forty yet, either, so who's to say I'll get to keep it?

My type: a big outdoorsy galoot, more brawn than brains, more street smarts than book smarts. Someone who probably won't notice you were wearing a wedding ring until a few minutes ago.

Or, if he does, won't likely care.

"Like to dance, little lady?"

I'd spotted him earlier out of the corner of my eye, a cowboy type, my height or an inch or two more, but packing less weight. Long and lean, built to play wide receiver to my tight end.

And no, I never played football myself. Only watch it when a TV's showing it in a room I'm in. Never cared about sports, even as a boy. Had the size, had the quickness, and I got tired of hearing I should go out for this team, go out for that one.

It was a game. Why waste my time on a game?

And here was this wide receiver, hitting on a woman who'd declared herself to be mine. She tightened her grip on my arm, and I guessed she was liking the way this was shaping up. Two studs taking it to the lot out back, squaring off, then doing their best to kill each other. And she'd stand there watching, the blood singing in her veins, until it was settled and she went home with the winner.

No question he was ready to play. He'd sized me up half an hour ago, before she was in the picture. There's a type of guy who'll do that, check out a room, work out who he might wind up fighting and how he'd handle it. Could be I'd done some of that myself, getting the measure of him, guessing what moves he'd make, guessing what would work against him.

Or I could walk away from it. Turn my back on both of 'em, head out of the bar, take my act on down the road. Not that hard to find a place that'd sell you a shot of Cuervo and a beer to back it up.

Except, you know, I never do walk away from things. Just knowing I could don't mean I can.

"Oh, that's very kind of you," she said. "But we were just leaving. Perhaps another time."

Getting to her feet as she said it, using just the right tone of voice, so as to leave no doubt that she meant it. Not cold, not putting him down, but nowhere near warm enough to encourage the son of a bitch.

Handled it just right, really.

I left my beer where it was, left my change there to keep it company. She took hold of my arm on the way out. There were some eyes on us as we left, but I guess we were both used to that.

When we hit the parking lot I was still planning the fight. It wasn't going to happen, but my mind was working it out just the same.

Funny how you'll do that.

You want to win that kind of a fight, what you want to do is get the first punch in. Before he sees it coming. First you bomb Pearl Harbor, then you declare war.

Let him think you're backing out of it, even. *Hey, I don't want to fight you!* And, when he's afraid you're gonna chicken out, you give him your best shot. Time it right, take him by surprise, and one punch is all you need.

Wouldn't have done that with old Lash LaRue, though. Oh, not because it wouldn't have done the job. Would have worked just fine, put him face-down on the gravel, Wranglers and snap-fastened dude shirt and silly pompadour and all.

But that'd cheat her out of the fight she was hoping to see.

So what I'd have done, once we're outside and good to go, was spread my hands in a can't-we-work-this-out gesture, leaving it for him to sucker-punch me. But I'd be ready, even though I wouldn't look ready, and I'd duck when he swung. They're always headhunters, dudes like him, and I'd be ducking almost before he was swinging, and I'd bury a fist midway between his navel and his nuts.

I'd do the whole deal with body shots. Why hurt your hands bouncing 'em off jawbone? Tall as he was, there was a whole lot of middle to him, and that's where I'd hammer him, and the first shot would take the fight out of him, and the starch out of his punches, if he even got to throw a second one.

I'd be aiming lefts at his liver. That's on the right, pretty much on the belt line. It's a legal punch in a boxing ring, never mind a parking lot, and if you find the spot it's a one-punch finisher. I haven't done it, or seen it done, but I believe it would be possible to kill a man with a liver shot.

But I was running the script for a fight that wasn't gonna happen, because my blonde had already written her own script and it turned out there wasn't a fight scene in it. Sort of a pity, in a way, because there'd have been a certain satisfaction in taking that cowboy apart, but his liver would live to fight another day. Any damage it sustained would be from the shots and beers he threw at it, not from any fists of mine.

And, you know, that would have been too easy, if all she was after was getting two roughnecks to duke it out over her. She had something a lot worse in mind.

"I hope I wasn't out of line," she said. "Getting us out of there. But I was afraid."

She hadn't seemed afraid.

"That you'd hurt him," she explained. "Kill him, even."

Her car was a Ford, the model the rental outfits were apt to give you. It was tucked between a pair of pickups, both of them showing dinged fenders and a lot of rust. She pressed a button to unlock the doors, and the headlights winked.

I played the gentleman, tagging along at her side, reaching to open the driver's side door for her. She hesitated, turned toward me, and it would have been a hard cue to miss.

I took hold of her and kissed her.

And yes, it was there, the chemistry, the biology, whatever you want to call it. She kissed back, and started to push her hips forward, then stopped herself, then couldn't stop herself. I felt the warmth of her through her jeans and mine, and I thought of doing her right there, just throwing her down and doing her on the gravel, with the two pickups screening us from view. Throw her a fast hard one, pull out and stand up while she's still quivering, and be out of there before she can get her game up and running.

Goodbye, little lady, because we just did what we came here to do, so whatever you've got to say, well, why do I have to listen to it?

I let go of her. She slipped behind the wheel, and I walked around the car and got in next to her. She started the engine but paused before putting the Ford in gear.

She said, "My name's Claudia."

Maybe it was and maybe it wasn't.

"Gary," I said.

"I don't live around here."

Neither did I. Don't live anywhere, really. Or, looking at it from another way, I live everywhere.

"My motel is just up the road. Maybe half a mile."

She waited for me to say something. What? *Are the sheets clean? Do they get HBO?*

I didn't say anything.

"Should we pick up something to drink? Because I don't have anything in the room."

I said I was fine. She nodded, waited for a break in the traffic, pulled onto the road.

I paid attention to the passing scenery, so I'd be able to come back for my car. A quarter mile down the road she took her right hand off the wheel and put it on my crotch. Her eyes never left the road. Another quarter mile and her hand returned to the wheel.

Had to wonder what was the point of that. Making sure I had something for her? Keeping me from forgetting why we were going to the motel?

Maybe just trying to show me she was every inch a lady.

I suppose I just keep on getting what I keep on looking for.

Because, face it, you don't go prospecting for Susie Homemaker in a lowdown joint with a lot full of pickups and hogs. Walk into a room where you hear Kitty Wells singing how it wasn't God who made honky-tonk angels, well, what are you gonna find but a honky-tonk angel yourself?

You want a one-man woman, you want someone who'll keep house and buy into the whole white-picket-fence trip, there's other places you can go hunting.

And I wasn't showing up at Methodist socials, or meetings of Parents Without Partners, or taking poetry workshops at a continuing education program. I was—another song—looking for love in all the wrong places, so why blame fate for sending me a woman like Claudia?

Or whatever her name was.

The motel was a one-story non-chain number, presentable enough, but not where a woman like her would stay if all she wanted was a place to sleep. She'd pick a Ramada or a Hampton Inn, but what we had here was your basic no-tell motel. Clean enough, and reasonably well maintained, and set back from the road for privacy. Her unit was around the back, where the little Ford couldn't be seen from the road. If it wasn't a rental, if it was her own car, well, no one driving by could spot the plate.

Like it mattered.

Inside, with the door shut and the lock set, she turned to me and for the first time looked the least bit uncertain. Like she was trying to think what to say, or waiting for me to say something.

Well, the hell with that. She'd already groped my crotch in the car, and that ought to be enough to break the ice. I reached for her and kissed her, and I got one hand on her ass and drew her in close.

I could have peeled those jeans off of her, could have ripped that fine silk blouse. I had the impulse.

More, I wanted to do some damage. Soften her up with a fist in her belly, see what a liver shot would do to her.

Fact: I have thoughts like that. They'll come to me, and when they do I always get a quick flash of my mother's face. Just the quickest flash, like the flash of green you'll sometimes get when you watch the sun go down over water. It's gone almost before it registers, and afterward you can't quite swear that you really saw it.

Like that.

I was gentle with her. Well, gentle enough. She didn't pick me out of the crowd because she wanted tender words and butterfly kisses. I gave her what I sensed she wanted, but I didn't take her any further than she wanted to go. It wasn't hard to find her rhythm, wasn't hard to build her up and hold her back and then let it all happen for her, staying with her all the way, coaxing the last little quiver out of the sweet machinery of her body.

Nothing to it, really. I'd been taught young. I knew what to do and how to do it.

"I knew it would be good."

I was lying there, eyes closed. I don't know what I'd been thinking about. Sometimes my mind just wanders, goes off by itself somewhere and thinks its own thoughts, and then a car backfires or something changes the energy in the room, and I'm back where I was, and whatever I was thinking about is gone without a trace.

Must be like that for everybody, I suppose. Can't be that I'm that special, me and my private thoughts.

This time it was her voice, bringing the present back as sure as a thunderclap. I rolled over and saw she was half-sitting in the bed beside me. She'd taken the pillow from under her ass and had it supporting her head and shoulders.

She had the air of a woman smoking a cigarette, but she wasn't a smoker and there weren't any cigarettes around. But it was like that, the cigarette afterwards, whether or not there was a cigarette in the picture.

"All I wanted," she said, "was to come in here and close a door and shut the world out, and then make everything in the world go away."

"Did it work?"

"Like magic," she said. "You didn't come."

"No."

"Was there something—"

"Sometimes I hold back."

"Oh."

"It makes the second time better. More intense."

"I can see how it would. But doesn't it take remarkable control?"

I hadn't been trying to hold back. I'd been trying to throw her a fuck she wouldn't quickly forget, that's all. But I didn't need to tell her all that.

"We'll be able to have a second time, won't we? You don't have to leave?"

"I'll be here all night," she said. "We can even have breakfast in the morning, if you'd like."

"I thought you might have to get home to your husband."

Her hands moved, and the fingers of her right hand fastened on the base of her ring finger, assuring themselves there was no ring there.

"Not the ring," I said. "The mark of the ring. A depression in the skin, because you must have taken it off just before you came into the roadhouse. And the thin white line, showing where the sun don't shine."

"Sherlock Holmes," she said.

She paused so that I could say something, but why help her out? I waited, and she said, "You're not married."

"No."

"Have you ever been?"

"Same answer."

She held her hand up, palm out, as if to examine her ring. I guess she was studying the mark where it had been.

She said, "I thought I'd get married right after high school. Where I grew up, if you were pretty, that's what happened. Or if you weren't pretty, but if somebody got you pregnant anyway."

"You were pretty."

She nodded. Why pretend she didn't know it? "But I wasn't pregnant, and this girlfriend got this idea, let's get out of this town, let's go to Chicago and see what happens. So just like that I packed a bag and we went, and it took her three weeks to get homesick and go right back."

"But not you."

"No, I liked Chicago. Or I thought I did. What I liked was the person I got to be in Chicago, not because it was Chicago but because it wasn't home."

"So you stayed."

"Until I went someplace else. Another city. And I had jobs, and I had boyfriends, and I spent some time between boyfriends, and it was all fine. And I thought, well, some women have husbands and children, and some don't, and it looks like I'll be one of the ones who don't."

I let her talk but didn't listen too closely. She met this man, he wanted to marry her, she thought it was her last chance, she knew it was a mistake, she went ahead and did it anyway. It was her story, but hardly hers alone. I'd heard it often enough before.

Sometimes I suppose it was true. Maybe it was true this time, far as that goes.

Maybe not.

When I got tired of hearing her I put a hand on her belly and stroked her. Her sudden intake of breath showed she wasn't expecting it. I ran my hand down, and her legs parted in anticipation, and I put my hand on her and fingered her. Just that, just lay beside her and worked her with my fingers. She'd closed her eyes, and I watched her face while my fingers did what they did.

"Oh! Oh! *Oh!*"

I got hard doing this, but didn't feel the need to do anything about it. After she came I just lay where I was. I closed my eyes and got soft again and lay there listening to all the silence in the room.

My father moved away when I was still in diapers. At least that was what I was told. I don't remember him, and I'm not convinced he was there. Somebody got her pregnant, it wasn't the Holy Ghost, but did he ever know it? Did she even know his last name?

So I was raised by a single mother, though I don't recall hearing the term back then. Early on she brought men home, and then she stopped doing that. She might come home smelling of where she'd been and what she'd been doing, but she'd come home alone.

Then she stopped that, too, and spent her evenings in front of the TV.

One night we were watching some program, I forget what, and she said, "You're old enough now. I suppose you touch yourself."

I knew what she meant. What I didn't know was how to respond.

She said, "Don't be ashamed. Everybody does it, it's part of growing up. Let me see it." And, when confusion paralyzed me, "Take off your pajama bottoms and show me your dick."

I didn't want to. I did want to. I was embarrassed, I was excited, I was . . .

"It's getting bigger," she said. "You'll be a man soon. Show me how you touch yourself. Look how it grows! This is better than television. What do you think about when you touch it?"

Did I say anything? I don't believe I did.

"Titties?" She opened her robe. "You sucked on them when you were a baby. Do you remember?"

Wanting to look away. Wanting to stop touching myself.

"I'll tell you a secret. Touching your dick is nice but it's nicer when someone else touches it for you. See? You can touch my titties while I do this for you. Doesn't that feel good? Doesn't it?"

I shot all over her hand. Thought she'd be angry. She put her hand to her face, licked it clean. Smiled at me.

"I don't know," she said.

Claudia, my blonde. I'd wondered, without much caring, just how natural that blondeness might be. Still an open question, because the hair on her head was the only hair she had.

Had to wonder what my mother would have made of that. Shaving her legs was her concession to femininity, and one she accepted grudgingly.

Got so she'd have me do it. Come out of the bath, all warm from the tub, and I'd spread lather and wield the safety razor. I'd be growing whiskers in a couple of years, she told me. Might as well get in some practice for a lifetime of shaving.

I asked Claudia what she didn't know.

"I just wanted an adventure," she said.

"Shut the world out. Keep it on the other side of that door."

"But you've got a power," she said. "The same thing that drew me to you, pulled me right across the room to where you were standing, it scares me."

"Why's that?"

She closed her eyes, chose her words carefully. " 'What happens here, stays here.' Isn't that how it works?"

"Like Las Vegas?"

She opened her eyes, looked into mine. "I've done this sort of thing before," she said.

"I'm shocked."

"Not as often as you might think, but now and then."

"When the moon's full?"

"And left it behind me when I drove away. Like a massage, like a spa treatment."

"Then home to hubby."

"How was it hurting him? He never knew. And I was a better wife to him for having an outlet."

Taking her time getting to it. It was like watching a baseball pitcher going through an elaborate windup. Kind of interesting when you already knew what kind of curveball to expect.

"But this feels like more than that, doesn't it?"

She gave me a long look, like she wanted to say yes but was reluctant to speak the words.

Oh, she was good.

"You've thought of leaving him."

"Of course. But I have . . . oh, how to say this? He gives me a very comfortable life."

"That generally means money."

"His parents were wealthy," she said, "and he was an only child, and they're gone, and it's all come to him."

"I guess the Ford's a rental."

"The Ford? Oh, the car I'm driving. Yes, I picked it up at the airport. Why would you—oh, because I probably have a nicer car than that. Is that what you meant?"

"Something like that."

"We have several cars. There's a Lexus that I usually drive, and he bought me a vintage sports car as a present. An Aston Martin."

"Very nice."

"I suppose. I enjoyed driving it at first, the power, the responsiveness. Now I rarely take it out of the garage. It's an expensive toy. As am I."

"His toy. Does he take you out and play with you much?"

She didn't say anything.

I put my hand where she didn't have any hair. Not stroking her, just resting it there. Staking a claim.

I said, "If you divorced him—"

"I signed one of those things."

"A pre-nup."

"Yes."

"You'd probably get to keep the toys."

"Maybe."

"But the lush life would be over."

A nod.

"I suppose he's a lot older than you."

"Just a few years. He seems older, he's one of those men who act older than their years, but he's not that old."

"How's his health?"

"It's good. He doesn't exercise, he's substantially overweight, but he gets excellent reports at his annual physical."

"Still, anybody can stroke out or have a heart attack. Or a drunk driver runs a red light, hits him broadside."

"I don't even like to talk about something like that."

"Because it's almost like wishing for it."

"Yes."

"Still," I said, "it'd be convenient, wouldn't it?"

*　　　*　　　*

It wasn't like that with my mother. A stroke, a heart attack, a drunk driver. There one day and gone the next.

Not like that at all.

Two, three years after she showed me how much nicer it was to have someone else touch me. Two, three years when I went to school in the morning and came straight home in the afternoon and closed the door on the whole world.

She showed me all the things she knew. Plus things she'd heard or read about, but never done.

And told me how to be with girls. "Like it's a sport and I'm your coach," she said. What to say, how to act, and how to get them to do things, or let me do things.

Then I'd come home and tell her about it. In bed, acting it out, fooling around.

Two, three years. And she started losing weight, and lost color in her face, and I must have noticed but it was day by day, and I was never conscious of it. And then I came home one day and she wasn't there, but there was a note, she'd be home soon. And an hour later she came in and I saw something in her face and I knew, but I didn't know what until she told me.

Ovarian cancer, and it had spread all through her, and they couldn't do anything. Nothing that would work.

Because of where it started, she wondered if it was punishment. For what we did.

"Except that's crap and I know it's crap. I was brought up believing in God, but I grew out of it, and I never raised you that way. And even if there was a God he wouldn't work it that way. And what's wrong with what we did? Did it hurt anybody?"

And a little later, "All they can give me is chemo and all it'll do is hurt like fury and make my hair fall out and maybe stretch my life a few months longer. My sweet baby boy, I don't want you remembering a jaundiced old lady dying by inches and going crazy with the pain. I don't want to hang around that long, and you have to help me get out."

School. I didn't play sports, I didn't join clubs, I didn't have friends. But I knew who sold drugs, everybody knew that much. Anything you wanted, and what I wanted was downs, and that was easy.

She wanted to take them when I left for school, so that I'd be gone when it happened, but I talked her out of that. She took them at night, and I lay beside her and held her hand while sleep took her. And I stayed there, so I could tell when her breathing stopped, but I couldn't stay awake, I fell asleep myself, and when I woke up around dawn she was gone.

I straightened the house, went into my room and made the bed look as though it had been slept in. Went to school and kept myself from thinking about anything. Went home, and turning my key in the lock I had this flash, expecting her to be walking around when I opened the door.

Yeah, right. I found her where I'd left her, and I called the doctor, said I'd left in the morning without wanting to disturb her. He could tell it was pills, I could tell he could tell, but he wanted to spare me, said it was her heart giving out suddenly, said it happened a lot in cases like hers.

If she was alive, if she'd never gotten sick, I'd still be living there. With the two of us in that house, and the whole rest of the world locked out of it.

She said, "I can't pretend I never thought about it. But I never wished for it. He's not a bad man. He's been good to me."

"Takes good care of you."

"He cleans his golf clubs after he plays a round. Has this piece of flannel he uses to wipe the faces of the irons. Takes the cars in for their scheduled maintenance. And yes, he takes good care of me."

"Maybe that's all you want."

"I was willing to settle for it," she said.

"And now you're not?"

"I don't know," she said, and put her hand on me. For just a moment it was another hand, a firm but gentle hand, and I was a boy again. Just for an instant, and then that passed.

And she went on holding me, and she didn't say anything but I could hear her voice in my head as clearly as if she'd spoken. *Willing to settle? Not anymore, my darling, because I've met you, and my world has changed forever. If only something could happen to him and we could be together forever. If only—*

"You want me to kill him," I said.

"Oh my God!"

"Isn't that where you were headed?"

She didn't answer, breathed deeply in and out, in and out. Then she said, "Have you ever—"

"Government puts you in a uniform, gives you a rifle, sends you halfway around the world. Man winds up doing a whole lot of things he might never do otherwise."

All of which was true, I suppose, but it had nothing much to do with me. I was never in the service.

Went to sign up once. You drift around, different things start looking good to you. Army shrink asked me a batch of questions, heard something he didn't like in my answers, and they thanked me for my time and sent me on my way.

Have to say that man was good at his job. I wouldn't have liked it there, and they wouldn't have liked me much, either.

*   *   *

She found something else to talk about, some rambling story about some neighbor of hers. I lay there and watched her lips move without taking in what she was saying.

Why bother? What she wasn't saying was more to the point.

Pleased with herself, I had to figure. Because she'd managed to get where she wanted to go without saying the words herself. Played it so neatly that I brought it up for her.

Like, I'm two steps ahead of you, Missy. Knew where you were going, saw what a roundabout route you had mapped out for yourself, figured I'd save us some time.

Better now, looking without listening. And it was like I couldn't hear her if I wanted to, all I could hear was her voice speaking in my head, telling me what I knew she was thinking. How we could be together for the rest of our lives, how I was all she wanted and all she needed, how we'd have a life of luxury and glamour and travel. Her voice in my head, drawing pictures of her idea of my idea of paradise.

Voices.

She moved, lay on her side. Stopped talking, and I stopped hearing that other voice, and she ran a hand the length of my body. And kissed my face and my neck, and worked her way south.

Yeah, right. To give me a hint of the crazy pleasures on offer once her husband was dead and buried. Because every man loves that, right?

Thing is, I don't. Not since another woman took the pills I'd bought her and didn't wake up.

One time, I had this date with a girl in my class. And she's coaching me.

You can get her to suck it. She'll still be a virgin, she can't get pregnant from it, and she'll be making you happy. Plus deep down she's plain dying

to do it. But what you want to do is help her out, tell her when she's doing
something wrong. Like you'll be her coach, you know?

Then she was gone, and since then I don't like having anybody doing that to me.

That army shrink? I guess he knew his business.

Still, she got it hard.

It plays by its own rules, doesn't it? The blood flows there or it
doesn't, and you can't make it happen or keep it from happening.
Didn't mean I enjoyed it, didn't mean I wanted her to keep it up.
More she did it, less I liked it.

Took hold of her head, moved her away.

"Is something wrong?"

"My turn," I said, and spread her out on the bed, and tucked a
pillow under her ass, and stuck a finger in to make sure she was wet.
Stuck the finger in her mouth, gave her a taste of herself.

Got on her, rode her long and hard, long and hard. She had one of
those rolling orgasms that won't quit, on and on and on, the gift that
keeps on giving.

I don't know where my mind was while this was going on. Off
somewhere, tuned in to something else. Watching HBO while she
was getting fucked on Showtime.

When she was done I just stayed where I was, on her and in her.
Looked down at her face, jaw slack, eyes shut, and saw what I hadn't
seen earlier.

That she looked like a pig. Just had a real piggish quality to her
features. Never saw it before.

Funny.

Her eyes opened. And her mouth started running, telling me it
had never been like this before.

"Did you—"

"Not yet."

"My God, you're still hard! Is there anything—"

"Not just yet," I said. "Something I'd like to know first. When you walked into the bar?"

"A lifetime ago," she said. And relaxed into what she thought was going to be a stroll down Memory Lane. How we met, how we fell in love without a word being spoken.

I said, "What I wondered. How did you know?"

"How did I—"

"How'd you know I was the one man in there who'd be willing to kill your husband for you?"

Eyes wide. Speechless.

"What did you see? What did you think you saw?"

And my hips started working, slowly, short strokes.

"Had it all worked out in your mind," I said. I moved my elbows so they were on her shoulders, pinning her to the bed, and my hands found her neck, circled it.

"So you'd be out of town, maybe pick up some other lucky guy to make sure you'd have an alibi. Get off good with him, because all the while you're thinking about how I'm doing it, killing your husband. Wondering exactly how I'm doing it, am I using a gun, a knife, a club? And you think of me doing him with my bare hands and that's what really gets you off, isn't it? Isn't it?"

She was saying something, but I couldn't hear it. Couldn't have heard a thunderclap, couldn't have heard the world ending.

"Filling my head with happily ever after, but once he's gone you don't need me anymore, do you? Maybe you'd find another sucker, get him to take me off the board."

Thrusting harder now. And my hands tightening on her throat. The terror in her eyes, Jesus, you could taste it.

Then the light went out of her eyes, and just like that she was gone.

Three, four more strokes and I got where I was going. What's funny is I didn't really feel it. The machinery worked, and I emptied myself into her, but you couldn't call it sensational, because, see, there wasn't a whole lot of sensation involved. There was a release, and that felt good, the way a piss does when you've been walking around with a full bladder.

Fact is, it's like that more often than not. I'd say the army shrink could explain it, but let's not make him into a genius. All he knew was the army was better off without me.

Most anybody's better off without me.

Claudia, for sure. Lying there now with her throat crushed and her eyes glassy. Minute I laid eyes on her, I knew she had the whole script worked out in her mind.

How'd she know? How'd she pick me?

And if I knew all that, if I could read her script and figure out a different ending than the one she had in mind, why'd I buy her a drink? All's said and done, how much real choice did I have in the matter once she'd gone and laid her hand on my arm?

Time to leave this town now, but who was I kidding? I'd find the same thing in the next town, or the town after that. Another roadhouse, where I might have to fight a guy or might not, but either way I'd walk out with a woman. She might not look as fine as this one, and she might have more hair besides what she had on her head, but she'd have the same plans for me.

And if I stayed out of the bars? If I went to some church socials, or Parents Without Partners, or some such?

Might work, but I wouldn't count on it. My luck, I'd wind up in the same damn place.

Like I said, I really know how to pick 'em.

Autumn at the Automat

The hat made a difference.

If you chose your clothes carefully, if you dressed a little more stylishly than the venue demanded, you could feel good about yourself. When you walked into the Forty-second Street cafeteria, the hat and coat announced that you were a lady. Perhaps you preferred their coffee to what they served at Longchamps. Or maybe it was the bean soup, as good as you could get at Delmonico's.

Certainly it wasn't abject need that led you to the cashier's window at Horn & Hardart. No one watching you dip into an alligator handbag for a dollar bill could think so for a minute.

The nickels came back, four groups of five. No need to count them, because the cashier did this and nothing else all day long, taking dollars, dispensing nickels. This was the Automat, and the poor girl was the next thing to an Automaton.

You took your nickels and assembled your meal. You chose a dish, put your nickels in the slot, turned the handle, opened the little window, and retrieved your prize. A single nickel got you a cup of coffee. Three more bought a bowl of the legendary bean soup, and another secured a little plate holding a seeded roll and a pat of butter.

You carried your tray to the counter, moving very deliberately, positioning yourself in front of the compartmented metal tray of silverware.

The moment you'd walked through the door you knew which table you wanted. Of course someone could have taken it, but no one did. Now, after a long moment, you carried your tray to it.

She ate slowly, savoring each spoonful of the bean soup, glad she'd decided against making do with a cup for the sake of saving a nickel. Not that she hadn't considered it. A nickel was nothing much, but if she saved a nickel twice a day, why, that came to three dollars a month. More, really. Thirty-six dollars and fifty cents a year, and that *was* something.

Ah, but she couldn't scrimp. Well, she could in fact, she had to, but not when it came to nourishing herself. What was that expression Alfred had used?

Kishke gelt. Belly money, money saved by cheating one's stomach. She could hear him speak the words, could see the curl of his lip.

Better, surely, to spend the extra nickel.

Not for fear of Alfred's contempt. He was beyond knowing or caring what she ate or what it cost her.

Unless, as she alternately hoped and feared, it didn't all stop with the end of life. Suppose that fine mind, that keen intelligence, that wry humor, suppose it had survived on some plane of existence even when all the rest of him had gone into the ground.

She didn't really believe it, but sometimes it pleased her to entertain the notion. She'd even talk to him, sometimes aloud but more often in the privacy of her mind. There was little she hadn't been able to share with him in life, and now his death had washed away what few conversational inhibitions she'd had. She could tell him anything now, and when it pleased her she could invent answers for him and fancy she heard them.

Sometimes they came so swiftly, and with such unsparing candor, that she had to wonder at their source. Was she making them up? Or was he no less a presence in her life for having left it?

Perhaps he hovered just out of sight, a disembodied guardian angel. Watching over her, taking care of her.

And no sooner did she have the thought than she heard the reply. *Watching is as far as it goes, liebchen. When it comes to taking care, you're on your own.*

She broke the roll in two, spread butter on it with the little knife. Put the buttered roll on the plate, took up the spoon, took a spoonful of soup. Then another, and then a bite of the roll.

She ate slowly, using the time to scan the room. Just over half the tables were occupied. Two women here, two men there. A man and woman who looked to be married, and another pair, at once animated but awkward with each other, whom she guessed were on a first or second date.

She might have amused herself by making up a story about them, but let her attention pass them by.

The other tables held solitary diners, more men than women, and most of them with newspapers. Better to be here than outside, as the city slipped deeper into autumn and the wind blew off the Hudson. Drink a cup of coffee, read the *News* or the *Mirror*, pass the time . . .

The manager wore a suit.

So did most of the male patrons, but his looked to be of better quality, and more recently pressed. His shirt was white, his necktie of a muted color she couldn't identify from across the room.

She watched him out of the corner of her eye.

Alfred had taught her to do this. Your eyes looked straight in front of you, and you didn't move them around to study the object of your interest. Instead you used your mind, telling it to pay attention to something on the periphery of your vision.

It took practice, but she'd had plenty of that. She remembered a lesson in Penn Station, across from the Left Luggage window. While she kept her eyes trained on the man checking his suitcase, Alfred had quizzed her on passengers queuing for the Philadelphia train. She described them in turn and glowed when he praised her.

The manager, she noted now, had a small, thin-lipped mouth. His wing tip shoes were brown, and buffed to a high polish. And, even as she observed him without looking at him, he studied his patrons in quite the opposite manner, his gaze moving deliberately, aggressively, from one table to the next. It seemed to her that some of her fellow diners could feel it when he stared at them, shifting uncomfortably without consciously knowing why.

She had prepared herself, but when his eyes found her she couldn't keep from drawing a breath, barely resisting the impulse to swing her eyes toward his. Her face darkened, she could feel it change expression, and when she reached for her coffee cup she could feel the tremor in her hand.

There he stood, beside the door to the kitchen, his hands clasped behind his back, his visage stern. There he stood, observing her directly while she observed him as she'd been taught.

There he was. With just a little effort, she managed to take a sip of coffee without spilling any of it. Then she returned the cup to the saucer, and took another breath.

And what did she suppose he had seen?

She thought of a half-remembered poem, one they'd read in English class. Something about wishing for the power to see oneself as one was seen by others. But what was the poem and who was its author?

What the restaurant manager would have seen, she thought, was a small and unobtrusive woman of a certain age, wearing good clothes that were themselves of a certain age. A decent hat that had largely lost its shape, an Arnold Constable coat, worn at the cuffs, with one of its original bone buttons replaced with another that didn't quite match.

Good shoes, plain black pumps. Her alligator bag. Both well crafted of good leather, both purchased from good Fifth Avenue shops.

And both showing their age.

As indeed was she, like everything she owned.

What would he have seen? The very picture of shabby gentility, she thought, and while she could not quite embrace the label, neither could she take issue with it. If her garments were shabby, they nevertheless announced unequivocally that their owner was genteel.

A man at the table immediately to her right—dark suit, gray fedora, napkin tucked into his collar to shield his tie—was alternating between sips of his coffee and forkfuls of his dessert, which looked to be apple crisp. She'd given no thought to dessert, and now a glimpse of it ignited the desire. She couldn't remember the last time she'd had their apple crisp, but she remembered how it tasted, a perfect balance of tart and sweet, the crisp part all sugary and crunchy.

They didn't always have apple crisp, which argued for her having a portion now, while it was available. It wouldn't cost her more than three nickels, four at the most, and she still had fifteen of the twenty nickels the cashier had supplied. All she had to do was walk to the dessert section at the far right and claim her prize.

No.

No, because her cup of coffee was almost gone, and she'd want a fresh cup to accompany her dessert. And that would only cost a single nickel more, and she could afford that even as she could afford the dessert itself, but even so the answer was—

No.

The word again, in Alfred's voice this time.

You are stalling, Knuddelmaus. It's not the pleasure of the sweet that lures you. It's the desire to postpone that which you fear.

She had to smile. If some corner of her own imagination was supplying Alfred's dialogue, it was doing so with great skill. *Knuddelmaus* had been one of his pet names for her, but he had used it infrequently, and it hadn't crossed her conscious mind in ages. Yet there it was, in his voice, bracketed with English words full of the flavor of the Ku'damm.

You know me too well, she said, speaking the words only in her mind. And she waited for what he might say next, but nothing more came. He was done for now.

Well, he'd said what he had to say. And he was right, wasn't he?

Robert Burns, she thought. A Scotsman, writing in dialect sure to baffle high school students, and she'd lost the rest of the poem but the one couplet had come back to her:

> *O wad some Power the giftie gie us*
> *To see oursels as ithers see us!*

But really, she wondered, would anyone in her right mind really want such a power?

The man with the gray fedora put down his fork and freed his napkin from his collar, using it to wipe the crumbs of his apple crisp from his lips. He picked up his coffee cup, found it empty, and moved to push back his chair.

But then he changed his mind and returned to his newspaper.

She fancied she could read his mind. The restaurant was not full, and no one was waiting for his table. He'd given them quite enough money—for his chicken pot pie and his coffee and his apple crisp—to keep his table as long as he wanted it. They didn't rush you here, they seemed to recognize that they were selling not just food but shelter as well, and it was warm here and cold outside, and it's not as though anyone were waiting for him in his little room.

Or for her in hers. She lived a ten-minute walk away, in a residential hotel on East Twenty-eighth Street. Her room was tiny, but still a good value at five dollars a week, twenty dollars a month. She'd long ago positioned a doily on the nightstand to hide the cigarette burn that was a legacy of a previous tenant, and hung framed illustrations from magazines to cover the worst water stains on the walls. There was a carpet on the floor, sound if threadbare, and downstairs the lobby furniture might have seen better days, but didn't that make it a good match for the residents?

Shabby genteel.

Two tables away, a woman about her age spooned sugar into her half-finished cup of coffee.

Free nourishment, she thought. The sugar bowl was on the table and you could make your coffee as sweet as you wished. The manager, who watched everything, no doubt registered every spoonful, but didn't seem to object.

When she'd first begun drinking coffee, she took plenty of cream and sugar. Alfred had changed that, teaching her to take it black and unsweetened, and now that was the only way she could drink it.

Not that the man had lacked a sweet tooth. He'd had a favorite place in Yorkville with pastries he proclaimed the equal of Vienna's Café Demel, and paired his Punschkrapfen or Linzer torte with strong black coffee.

You must have the contrast, Liebchen. The bitter with the sweet. One taste strengthens the other. At the table as in the world.

His words were strongly accented now. *Vun taste strengsens ze uzzer.* When she'd met him he was new in the country, but even then his English held just a trace of Middle Europe, and within a year or two he'd polished away the last of it. He'd allowed it to return only when it was just the two of them, as if she alone was permitted to hear where he'd come from.

And it was when he talked about the past, about times in Berlin and Vienna, that it was strongest.

She took a last sip of coffee. It wasn't the equal to the strong dark brew he'd taught her to prefer, but it was certainly more than acceptable.

Did she want another cup?

Without shifting her gaze, she allowed herself another visual scan of the room, saw the manager look at her and then away, studied the woman whom she'd seen adding sugar to her coffee.

A woman dressed much as she was dressed, with a decent hat and a well-cut dove gray coat, neither of them new. A woman whose hair was graying and whose forehead showed worry lines, but whose mouth was still full-lipped and generous.

Now the woman was looking at her, studying her without knowing she was being studied in return.

Pick an ally, Schatzi. They come in handy.

She let her eyes move to meet the woman's, noted her embarrassment at the contact, and eased it with a smile. The woman smiled back, then turned her attention to her coffee cup. And, contact established, she picked up her own cup. It was empty, but no one could know that, and she took a little sip of nothing at all.

You are stalling, Knuddelmaus.

Well, yes, she was. It was warm in here and cold out there, but it would only grow colder as afternoon edged into evening. It wasn't the wind or the air temperature that made her reluctant to leave her table.

It was the fourth of the month, and her rent had been due on the first. She'd been late before, and knew that nobody would say anything until she was a week overdue. So there'd be a reminder in three days, a gentle advisory delivered with a gentle smile, directing her attention to what was surely an oversight.

She didn't know what the next step would be, or when it would come. So far that single reminder had achieved the desired effect, and she'd found the money and paid the monthly rental a day after it had been requested.

That time, she'd pawned a bracelet. Three stones, carnelian and lapis and citrine, half-round oval cabochons set in yellow gold. Thinking of it now, she looked down at her bare wrist.

It had been a gift of Alfred's, but that had been true of every piece of jewelry she'd owned. The bracelet was evidently her favorite, as it had been the last to make the trip to the pawnshop. She'd told herself she'd redeem it when the opportunity presented itself. She went on believing this until the day she sold the pawn ticket.

And by then she'd grown accustomed to no longer owning the bracelet, so the pain was muted.

We get used to things, Liebchen. A man can get used to hanging.

Could anyone speak those lines convincingly other than with the inflection of a Berliner?

And you are still stalling.

*　　*　　*

She put her handbag on the table, then was taken by a fit of coughing. She put her napkin to her lips, took a breath, coughed again.

She didn't look, but knew people were glancing in her direction.

She took a breath, managed not to cough. She was still holding her napkin, and now she picked up each of her utensils in turn, the soup spoon, the coffee spoon, the fork, the butter knife. She wiped them all thoroughly and placed each of them in her handbag. And fastened the clasp.

Now she did look around, and let something show on her face.

She got to her feet. Not for the first time, she felt a touch of dizziness upon standing. She put a hand on the table for support, and the dizziness subsided, as it always did. She drew a breath, turned, and walked toward the door.

She moved at a measured pace, deliberately, neither hurrying nor slowing. This Automat, unlike the one closer to her hotel, had a brass-trimmed revolving door, and she paused to let a new patron enter the restaurant. She thought about the desk clerk at her hotel, and the twenty dollars. Her purse held a five-dollar bull and two singles, along with those fifteen nickels, so she could pay a week's rent and have a few days to find the rest, and—

"Oh, I don't think so. Stop right there, ma'am."

She extended a foot toward the revolving door, and now a hand fastened on her upper arm. She spun around, and there he was, the thin-lipped manager.

"Bold as brass," he said. "By God, you're not the first person to walk off with the odd spoon, but you took the lot, didn't you? And polished them while you were at it."

"How dare you!"

"I'll just take that," he said, and took hold of her handbag.

"No!"

Now there were three hands gripping the alligator bag, one of his and two of her own. "How dare you!" she said again, louder this time, knowing that everyone in the restaurant was looking at the two of them. Well, let them look.

"You're not going anywhere," he told her. "By God, I was just going to take back what you stole, but you've got an attitude that's as bad as your thieving." He called over his shoulder: "Jimmy, call the precinct, tell the guy on the desk to send over a couple of boys." His eyes glinted—oh, he was enjoying this—and his words washed over her as he told her he would make an example of her, that a night or two in jail would give her more of a sense of private property.

"Now," he said, "are you gonna open that bag, or do we wait for the cops?"

There were two policemen, one a good ten years older than the other, though both looked young to her. And it was clear that neither of them wanted to be there, enlisted to punish a woman for stealing tableware from a cafeteria.

It was the elder of the two who told her, almost apologetically, that she'd have to open the bag.

"Certainly," she said, and worked the clasp, and took out the knife and the fork and both spoons. The policemen looked on with no change in expression, but the manager knew what he was seeing, and her heart quickened at the look on his face.

"I like the food at this restaurant," she said, "and the people who dine here are decent, and the chairs are comfortable enough. But as for your spoons and forks, I don't care for the way they feel in my hands or in my mouth. I prefer my own. These were my mother's, they're hallmarked sterling silver, you can see her monogram—"

*   *   *

The apology came in a rush, and found her unrelenting. It would be the manager's pleasure to give her a due bill entitling her to thus and so many meals absolutely without charge, and—

"I'm sure nothing could induce me to come here ever again."

Well, he was terribly sorry, and fortunately no actual harm had been done, so—

"You've humiliated me in front of a room full of people. You laid hands on me, you grabbed my arm, you tried to grab my purse." She glanced around. "Did you see what this man did?"

Several patrons nodded, including the woman who'd spooned all that sugar into her coffee.

More words of apology, but she cut right through them. "My nephew is an attorney. I think I should call him."

Something changed in the manager's face. "Why don't we go to my office," he suggested. "I'm sure we can work this out."

When she got back to her hotel, the first thing she did was pay her rent, the month that was overdue and the next two in advance.

Upstairs in her room, she took the knife and fork and spoons and returned them to her dresser drawer. They were part of a set, all mono-grammed with a capital J, but they had not been her mother's.

Nor were they sterling. Had they been, she'd have contrived to sell them. But they were decent silver plate, and while she did not cus-tomarily carry them around with her, they served admirably when she warmed up a can of baked beans on her hotplate.

And they'd served admirably today.

In his office, the manager had tried to buy his way out with a hun-dred dollars, and doubled it quickly when it was apparent he'd insult-ed her. A deep breath followed by a firm shake of her head had coaxed another hundred out of him, and she weighed that, hovering on the brink of accepting it, only to sigh and wonder if she wouldn't be best advised to call her nephew after all.

His offer jumped from three hundred to five hundred, and she had the sense he might well go higher, but Alfred had impressed upon her the folly of wringing every nickel out of a situation. So she didn't jump at it, but thought for a long moment and gave in gracefully.

He had her sign something. She didn't hesitate, jotting down a name she'd used before, and he counted out the appointed sum in twenty-dollar bills.

Twenty-five of them.

Or ten thousand nickels, Liebchen. If you want to give the cashier a heart attack.

"But it went well," she told Alfred, speaking the words aloud in the little room. "I pulled it off, didn't I?"

The answer to that was clear enough not to require his stating it. She hung her hat on the peg, her coat in the closet. She sat on the edge of the bed and counted her money, then tucked away all but one of the twenties where no one would think to look for them.

Alfred had schooled her in hiding money, even as he'd taught her how to get hold of it.

"I couldn't be sure it would work," she said. "It came to me one day. I had a fork with one bent tine, and I thought how low-quality their cutlery was, and I could imagine a woman, oh, one who'd come down a peg or two over time, bringing her own silverware in her purse. And then I forgot about her, and then she came back to me, and—"

And one thing led to another. And it had worked splendidly, and the nervousness she'd felt had been appropriate to the role she'd been playing. Now, seeing the incident from a distance, viewing it with Alfred's critical perspective, she could see ways to refine her performance, to make more certain the taking of the bait and the sinking of the hook.

Could she do it again? She wouldn't need to, not for quite a while. Her rent was paid through the end of the year, and the money she'd tucked away would keep her for that long and longer.

Of course she couldn't return to that particular Automat. There were others, including a perfectly nice one very near to her hotel, but did the chain's managers keep one another up to date? The man she'd dealt with, the man with the thin lips and the mean little eyes, had hardly covered himself with glory in their encounter, and you'd think he'd want to keep it to himself. But one never knew, and the less one left to chance—

Perhaps, for at least a while, she'd be well advised to take her custom elsewhere. There were many places nearby where the shabby genteel could dine decently at low cost. Childs, for example, had several restaurants, with a nice one nearby on Thirty-fourth Street, in the shadow of the Third Avenue El.

Or Schrafft's. The prices were a little higher there, and they drew a better class of customer, but she'd fit in well enough. And if one of them had the right sort of manager, she'd know what to do when her funds got low.

One had to adapt. She was too old to slip on a just-mopped floor at Gimbel's, too frail to stumble on an escalator, and there were all those routines Alfred had taught her, gambits you couldn't bring off without a partner.

Schrafft's, she decided. And she'd begin by scouting the one on West Twenty-third, in the heart of the Ladies' Mile.

Would they have apple crisp? She hoped so.

Gym Rat

I'd seen him at the gym. He worked Mondays and Thursdays with Troy, one of the better personal trainers on staff. Most of the men and women who use trainers let it go at that, and you never see them show up on their own. But this guy was there just about every day. Right around eleven he'd come out of the locker room in black Spandex, and he'd be on the floor for an hour, sometimes longer. Machines and free weights, the elliptical trainer, sometimes ten or twenty minutes on one of the bikes.

And you'd have to say it was working for him. He had to be a few years older than me, crowding forty, say. Right around six feet tall, and if his body wasn't one the gym would use in its ads, it was better than most. Decent musculature, pretty respectable definition. He didn't push himself that hard, and if he used a substance to give himself a boost, it wouldn't be anything edgier than a protein shake, and maybe a couple of caps of creatine. No way he was into 'roids.

Which is, no question, the best policy for most people. I'm a little different, I'm a fucking gym rat, and that means I'm in sweats or Spandex seven days a week, and generally for four or five hours at a time. When that's your life, of course you're going to experiment, see what works and what doesn't. And some things don't—you do a lot of juice, you're gonna wind up with a basketball sitting on your shoulders and a pair of raisins in your nutsack, and no way that's a good idea. But if you can keep things in proportion, well, you can put in longer hours and lift heavier weights and see real results, and someday you might wind up Governor of California. Better living through chemistry, you know?

Anyway, for a Mr. Natural in his age bracket he shaped up okay.

Then one Wednesday morning he asked me to spot him on the bench press.

You don't have to know someone all that well to ask for a spot. What it is, the designated spotter stands right behind you, ready to lend a hand if one's required. Well, two hands, really, to assist you in raising the bar for that final rep you're determined to grind out, and perhaps offer an encouraging word while he's at it. It's a way to achieve your best performance, because you can go all the way to failure.

Plus it's an important safety precaution. Every now and then you hear about some musclehead working out on his own, at home or in an empty gym, and he fails on the final rep and he can't get the bar off his chest. If he's stacked enough iron on it, it'll crush his chest and kill him.

I took my position, hands at the ready, and he did his dozen reps at 135 and put the bar back on the rack. He could have cranked out a few more, and a potted house plant could have done as much for him as I did.

"Thanks," he said.

I said it was no problem, or that he was welcome, or whatever I said, and he said, "We should talk."

Oh?

"But not here." He didn't look at me as he spoke, and his lips weren't moving much. I got the feeling this was a movie, and any minute now Matt Damon would race through, ready to kick ass.

"I've got a business proposition for you," he said. "There's a diner on the south side of Thirty-fourth Street a few doors west of Ninth Avenue. Do you know it?"

"I can probably find it."

"Why don't you find it at three o'clock this afternoon? It's quiet then. I'll be in a booth. Maybe you could take the booth right behind me."

Jesus, we were still in that movie.

I said, "Um, I don't know . . ."

"Just show up and listen," he said. "I'll pay you a hundred dollars just to hear me out. If you don't like what you hear, that's as far as it'll ever go."

He didn't wait for an answer, got up from the bench and headed for the dumbbell rack.

The hundred dollars, I decided, was just the right amount. Much less and I think I'd have passed, much more and I'd have been even more suspicious than I already was. Fifty bucks or two hundred, I'd have walked away from it.

Or would I? Easy to say what you would have done, but hard to know for a fact. Maybe I was intrigued. Maybe I'd have wanted to see how the movie came out.

Some geography, okay? The gym's in the Village, on the corner of West Twelfth Street and Greenwich Avenue. My room's a few blocks away in Chelsea, in an SRO on Seventeenth Street. And you know where to find the diner, Thirty-fourth just west of Ninth. The subway'll run you from Fourteenth to Thirty-fourth, or you can walk it in half an hour, forty minutes if you dawdle.

I took my time. I tend to be right on time, but if we were going to be playing Separate Tables I wanted him to be sitting at his when I walked in the door.

And he was, and he'd been there long enough to have a sandwich and a cup of coffee in front of him, and a bite gone from the sandwich.

I walked to his booth and past it, his eyes barely registering my presence. I sat down so we were back to back, which meant we'd miss out on eye contact but wouldn't have to raise our voices to be heard. I pretended to look at the menu, and when the waitress shuffled over I ordered an unsweetened iced tea.

When she'd walked off I heard him say, "Reach over your shoulder."

I did, and he put a piece of paper in my hand. It had Benjamin Franklin's picture on it, so I was now officially a hundred dollars ahead of the game, less whatever they charged me for the iced tea.

Walking uptown, I'd wondered if he was gay. He didn't give off that kind of a vibe, though God knows not everybody does. More to the point, the hundred dollars just to hear him out was way high for a sexual overture.

Well, I was here, and I'd taken the hundred. I'd know soon enough what it was all about.

"Reach over your shoulder."

Again? I did, and this time instead of Franklin I got a picture of a woman. She was sitting in a deck chair alongside a swimming pool, and wearing a bathing suit and dark glasses. She looked pretty enough, though the sunglasses made her face hard to read. Nice body.

"My wife," he said.

I thought, Oh, I get it. It was sex after all. He wanted me to fuck her. While he watched? Or some tag team thing he'd picked up from online porn?

I wished I could see his face. All I got this way was disembodied words, spoken in a soft voice, and it was hard to take their measure that way.

He said, "I worry about her."

He paused, and I waited, and *he* waited, evidently wanting me to say something. What I said was, "Oh?"

"I travel a lot on business. We live across the river in Jersey. A house, not an apartment. Anybody could break in. Nerissa could be the victim of a home invasion. She could be raped, killed."

Or struck by lightning, I thought. Or drowned in a flash flood.

"If you think she needs a bodyguard," I said, "I'm the wrong person. At a minimum you'd want someone with martial arts training, and probably firearms training as well."

"The last thing she needs is a bodyguard."

I didn't need to see his face when he spoke that line.

He let it sink in. I looked again at the photo of the nice-looking woman who didn't need a bodyguard.

"We have two children," he said. "A boy and a girl. They'll both be at summer camp for the entire month of August. That's in Maine, and Nerissa and I are going up to Bar Harbor for the last two weeks of the month. Nothing there you can't get cheaper and easier at the Jersey Shore, except for the clam rolls, but it makes a change, and then we pick up the kids and tip their counselors and drive home."

A long speech. It didn't seem to require a comment, so I didn't supply one.

"The second weekend in August," he said, "I've got a conference in Las Vegas. I go every year."

Okay.

"That's when I'm afraid it might happen."

"The home invasion," I said.

"Right."

"The rape and murder."

"The rape," he said, "would be optional."

How did he pick me? We'd never spoken, never had any interaction whatsoever. He must have seen me at the gym, even as I'd seen him, but what could he have spotted that let him believe I'd hire on to kill his wife? Did I flash gang signs? Sport aggressive tattoos? Glare at other gym members with murderous intensity?

No to all of that. Nor, assuming he'd done his research, could he have found anything in my résumé to make me a likely prospect. I'd never been arrested, let alone convicted of a crime. This was not to say I'd never broken the law, but any transgressions had gone unrecorded.

I led a simple life, and an inexpensive one. The rent for my furnished room was low. I didn't drink or smoke. I wore jeans and T-shirts from Old Navy or the Gap. My biggest expense was my gym membership, and that was limited to non-peak hours and consequently discounted.

On what basis had he selected me for this astonishing offer? It scarcely needed to be said that I'd never killed anyone. If I was not a complete stranger to violence, I couldn't remember the last time I'd been in a fight. It would have had to be in high school. Fifteen years ago, at a minimum.

For God's sake, why me?

"Seventy-five thousand dollars," he said.

Before he got to the price, he supplied the reason. The marriage had turned sour several years ago. He wanted out. If he divorced her, she'd fight tooth and nail for the children, and almost certainly get them. And she'd move them out of the state, she'd already threatened as much.

Simpler to kill her. Cheaper, too, considering what he'd save in legal fees and alimony. And satisfying, because he'd come to hate the woman, and would be happy to see her dead.

Jesus.

I said, "Do you even know my name?"

"No," he said, "and I don't want to. I don't want to know anything about you. My name is Graham Tillman, and—"

"I don't think you should tell me."

"You could hardly do this without knowing. How are you going to force your way into a house without knowing the name of its owner? And you already know my wife's name."

Nerissa, I thought. Had I ever known anyone with that name?

"Here's what we'll do," he was saying. "Right now it hardly matters which way you're leaning. You'll want to live with the thought for awhile and see where it goes. Today's Wednesday. Our paths may or may not cross at the gym tomorrow, but in any event we won't speak."

He'd be working with Troy, I thought.

"I won't be at the gym Friday," he said. "I have meetings throughout the day. One of them's with you, at the same hour as today. Three p.m."

"Here?"

"No. I'll never come back here, and I recommend you avoid it yourself. I've been unable to spot security cameras here, but even if they have them, we'd never be in the same frame. Even so, it would be the height of folly for us ever to meet twice in the same place."

He'd thought this through. That was reassuring, and at the same time it was unsettling.

"There's a similar establishment," he said, "at the southwest corner of Second Avenue and Seventy-second Street. I'm hardly ever in that neighborhood."

"Neither am I."

"Same drill as today. I'll be there at three. Take the adjacent booth."

"I don't really think—"

"That this is for you? Right now it's not important what you think. Take forty-eight hours to live with the notion. Whatever you decide, come to the restaurant."

"Why, if what I decide is to pass?"

"Same deal as today," he said, "except what you get for showing up is two hundred dollars. Don't say anything now. Get your check and go. I'll stay here another ten or fifteen minutes."

Tradecraft, I thought. I wonder how he knew all this stuff. Maybe we just both went to the same movies.

"You might let me have the photo back."

"Oh, right," I said.

The waitress had dropped off the check when she brought my iced tea. I'd only drunk half of it, but that was enough. I put some change next to my glass, carried the check to the register, paid it and left.

I just missed a bus heading down Ninth Avenue, and thought about a cab. I was a hundred dollars to the good, I could treat myself to a taxi, but wound up walking instead. And when I got to Seventeenth Street I kept on going and followed my feet back to the gym. I spent half an hour doing some lifts that hadn't been a part of my routine earlier that day, just to spend a few minutes in my body instead of my mind. I wrapped it up with ten minutes in the sauna and a few more under the shower, grabbed a protein shake on the way out, and got home in time for the TV news.

Drought here, flooding there, wildfires in California. Always something.

I stretched out on my bed and thought about the fresh hundred dollar bill in my wallet. Money wasn't something I spent a lot of time thinking about. I didn't need much, and something always turned up. When I was running short, I could pick up day work with a moving company, or take some bartender's shift behind the stick. And now and then one of my personal trainer friends would overbook himself and bring me in to pick up the slack.

And there were more marginal gigs that came my way, and sometimes I said yes and sometimes I passed. Tagging along and looking muscular when an entrepreneurial acquaintance wanted to collect a debt, or handle a transaction, or warn off a competitor.

I lay there and thought about the hundred dollars, which hadn't affected me much beyond making me consider a taxi. Still, I was better off with it than without it, and all I'd had to do for it was walk for half an hour and drink a glass of iced tea.

Friday I could pick up twice as much, but Seventy-second and Second was too far to walk. I'd have to take two subways, or a bus and a subway—or, I suppose, two buses.

Should I have objected to the meeting place? Told him to pick some place I could walk to? Beyond the logistics of the thing, a little assertiveness might have been appropriate.

Never mind. Proceed to Seventy-second and Second, pick up two hundred dollars.

And then what? He hadn't mentioned a city, but if he lived anywhere in New Jersey I could forget about walking there. To his house, to kill his wife.

What made him think I'd be up for something like that?

I went to bed early, slept like a dead man. I always do. Well, I don't drink, I don't smoke, I stay away from sugar and keep carbs down, and I'm done with my daily dose of coffee before I hit the gym. My body gets a good workout seven days a week, and there's rarely anything on my mind to keep it humming after hours. Why wouldn't I sleep well?

I had my coffee around the corner, walked to the gym, and stopped for breakfast across the street at the Village Den. Swiss cheese omelet, side of bacon, side of sausage. I didn't have to tell them to skip the bread and potatoes.

I worked heavy, concentrating on pecs and delts. Moved on to the treadmill, and I set the speed low enough so that I could have kept it up all day. I let my mind wander, the way it'll do.

Some of the members put themselves through long sessions on the cardio machines, but a lot of them are on and off in ten minutes. I was on a treadmill in a row of eight or nine treadmills, and right in front of us was a row of about as many elliptical trainers. When I started, the machine directly in front of me had the Pillsbury Doughboy on it, but he was gone before I broke a sweat. He was followed almost immediately by a woman wearing running shorts and a singlet, and beyond checking her out (nice little butt, good legs) I didn't pay any real attention to her.

But she stayed on her machine and I stayed on mine, and somewhere along the way I found myself thinking that this was her, Nerissa Tillman. That didn't make any sense, and there was nothing about her to implant the idea. All I'd seen of Tillman's wife was a palm-sized photo from the front, and all I was seeing of this woman was her legs and her butt and the back of her head. She had dark hair, and so did Nerissa Tillman, but so what?

I told my mind *Thanks for sharing*, and I kicked up the pace on the treadmill, figuring if my legs had to work a little harder it might give my mind a chance to chill. But it didn't really work, because I couldn't take my eyes off that cute little ass of hers, and I was getting hard looking at it.

She was still going when I finished my run and quit the treadmill. I managed to get a look at her, and of course she looked nothing like the photo. Just a fairly ordinary-looking woman, and she was probably at her best when viewed from the back, but even then she was nothing special, not really.

But that was kind of beside the point, wasn't it?

Thursday night I was supposed to meet a friend at a storefront chess club on Sullivan Street. A woman with an international ranking was scheduled to play a twenty-board exhibition, and Joel and I would be two of her opponents, paying twenty dollars each for the privilege. We figured it wouldn't take her too long to beat us, and then the two of us would have dinner at an Italian place we both liked.

I reached him on his cell, begged off. Something I got to do, I told him. The fee was already paid, and I said he could find someone else to take my place or just let it go.

Friday morning I got to the gym earlier than usual. I boosted poundages on all my lifts, did extra sets, capped each series with a static contraction rep. It felt like I had more energy than usual, but I don't know. I think it was more a case of having a need to use every bit of what energy I had.

Hell of a workout.

At 2:45 that afternoon I was in a small antique shop called Your Grandmother's Closet. I was the only customer, and I hoped the shopkeeper wasn't counting on me, because I was only there so I could look out the window. The diner where I was supposed to meet Graham Tillman was right across the street.

I took a moment to admire a pair of brass bookends, one with a bull, the other with a bear. A gift for a stockbroker, I suppose, though they'd work just as well for a person who just happened to like bronze animals. They were even heavier than they looked, and either one would put a pretty good dent in a person's skull.

I didn't say as much to the woman, a frail creature who was already a little bit afraid of me. A developed physique will have that effect on some people, and draw admiration or hostility from others, depending where they're coming from.

She had, she told me, quite a few other bookends besides the ones on display, some quite modestly priced. I could have told her there were only three books in my room, and they were doing fine stacked one on top of the other, but right about then a car pulled up at the corner and my guy got out of it.

"I'm just looking," I said. "Getting out of the heat for a minute or two. But bookends are a great gift, aren't they? When I need to buy somebody a present, I'll know where to come."

I didn't pay attention to her response. I watched Tillman do nothing at all until the light turned and the car drove off. Then he looked around guardedly, saw nothing to put him off stride, and went into the restaurant.

I'd spent enough time in the shop and went out onto the sidewalk. I stood in a patch of shade and watched him order from the menu. By the time the waiter brought him his food I'd crossed the street and entered the diner.

The booth behind him was empty, as was the one in front of him. I went straight to his booth, sat on the seat across from him.

His eyes widened.

I said, "I don't know that James Bond would do it this way, though I suppose it's a question of which actor was playing him. Sean Connery, now, he'd sit wherever he wanted."

"It seemed a useful precaution."

"Until someone notices that two men at different tables with their backs to each other are having a conversation. This way we're just two men having a meal."

While he thought that over the waiter came by with a menu, and I asked him to bring me an unsweetened iced tea. Did I want lemon? Sure, I said. Lemon'd be nice.

Tillman said, "Maybe you're right. But I'm the one who'll be in the hot seat. Something happens to a woman, they look at the husband. And they don't just eyeball him. They look at everything. They tear his life apart."

"You'll be able to prove you weren't around when it happened."

"But can I prove I wasn't *here*? When *this* happened?"

"In other words, they'll figure you hired somebody."

"And how do I set up an alibi for that?"

We kicked that around a little, and I reminded him he owed me two hundred dollars. For showing up. He gave me a pair of hundreds, and I took my time filing them away in my wallet.

He said, "I get the feeling you're not going to do it."

"Why do you say that?"

"Because sitting at separate tables was a sensible precaution, with no added risk, and you're bright enough to recognize that. But you'd already decided to turn me down, so there was suddenly no need for precautions. And you wanted to be able to see my face when you told me to forget it."

He was right that I wanted to see his face.

"There's something you probably don't know," he said. "It was too late for the papers, and I don't think it would get any TV play here in the city. But where I live it made the morning newscast."

"I think you said Jersey?"

"Morristown."

"And something happened there?"

He shook his head. "Something happened in Denville."

"I've heard of Morristown," I said, "but not Danville."

"Denville. With an E."

"Whatever. That's near where you are?"

"Ten, twelve miles away. Maybe fifteen minutes in light traffic."

He paused, waiting for me to ask what had happened in Denville. I figured he'd get there on his own.

"A woman was raped there," he said. "And murdered. A woman in a garden apartment, somebody broke in and did what he did."

"They catch the guy?"

"Not yet."

"They probably will," I said. "Sooner rather than later, would be my guess. A guy like that, he'll leave his DNA all over the place, get his fingerprints on every surface that'll take them. Then he shows up for work with scratches on his face and a story about his neighbor's hostile cat."

"Maybe they'll catch him."

"Maybe? Of course they will, and the sooner the better. You don't want assholes like that running free."

He gave me a look that was hard to read.

I said, "What?"

"Maybe it'll take them a while," he said. "Maybe they won't catch up with him until something else happens."

It was good being face to face with him, not back to back in separate booths. I had a chance to watch the play of expressions on his face, and after a moment I said, "Oh."

"Right."

I drank some of my iced tea. I said, "Same thing happens to another woman, they've got to think it might be the same guy."

"Opens things up, doesn't it?"

"They'll still grill you up and down," I said.

"Because it's always the husband."

"But you're in Vegas when it happens, and it's a fact that you could have hired it done, and the mope you hired could have decided to imitate a killing that just happened—"

"But it starts getting far-fetched, doesn't it? As opposed to the simple explanation that the same nut job raped and killed both women. In fact, who's to say he'll stop? Maybe he does another one, or even two or three, and *then* they catch him, and they hang every dead girl in the state around his neck before they ship him off to Rahway."

We batted it back and forth. I pointed out that the cops would hold back specifics of the Denville killing. Right now we didn't know what he'd used, a gun or a knife or his own two hands, and that might come out in follow-up stories, but there'd almost certainly be other things that wouldn't.

"If he left prints in Denville," I said, "they're not going to turn up in Morristown."

"So who says he can't learn from experience? He's more careful the second time around. Same thing with his DNA. I don't know if he used a condom in Denville, but my guess is he'll definitely use one with, um, the woman in Morristown."

Didn't want to say her name. Interesting.

"The big question is timing," he said. "Today is what, the twenty-second?"

Was it? That sounded about right. It was a Friday, it was in July, and it had been July for a while. The twenty-second was a reasonable date for it to be.

"A week from Sunday," he said, "camp starts."

"In Maine, I think you said."

"On the tenth, I fly out to Vegas. I'm there Wednesday, Thursday, Friday and Saturday nights. I fly back here on Sunday, that'd be the fourteenth, and Monday morning we're supposed to drive up to Bar Harbor."

Bah Hahbuh, that was how he said it, exaggerating the regional accent.

"If all goes well," I said.

"If all goes well," he said, "Bah Hahbuh can go fuck itself. You see the window we've got, don't you? Those four nights."

"The tenth through the thirteenth."

"If that nut job in Denville can stay out of custody between now and then—" He drew a breath, let it out. "Make it all a lot easier," he said.

I thought about it, nodded. Hard to see anything wrong with his reasoning.

"So he's got three weeks to stay away from the cops, and you've got three weeks to get ready."

"I never said I'd do it."

He wasn't expecting that, and his face showed it. I could see him replaying our conversation, confirming my failure to commit. "I jumped to a conclusion," he said. "You took the money—"

"The two hundred dollars. For showing up."

"Yes, of course. But the way you were talking, speculating about the lunatic in Denville—well, as I said, I jumped to a conclusion."

"There's something I need to know first."

"Oh?"

"Why me? You don't know me at all. The only time either of us said a word to the other was when you asked me to spot you on the bench press, and by then you'd already picked me out for the job, hadn't you?"

He thought it over, nodded.

"Who else did you ask?"

"Nobody."

"Are you sure of that? It's important, if you sounded out anybody else I really have to know."

"I'm absolutely certain. You were the only one."

I knew he was telling the truth, even as I'd known that would be his answer.

What I didn't know was why.

And how could I, when he didn't know himself? "I just had a feeling," he said.

"A feeling?"

"A sense, an impression, I don't know what else to call it. I had my eye on you for about a week."

"A week."

"Maybe ten days. I didn't stare, I was discreet, but I'd look for you every time I went to the gym. You were usually there."

"I'm there a lot."

"I didn't know anything about you," he said, "and I still don't. I don't suppose it would have been hard to find out your name, but I made a point of not doing so. A little voice in my head kept telling me you were the guy."

"The guy."

"The answer to my problem."

"And this just came to you."

"I don't know any better way to explain it."

And would I do it? The unspoken question hung in the air. He'd had two bites of his sandwich and hadn't touched it since I sat down. I'd had one small sip of my iced tea when the waiter brought it, and since then I'd wrapped my hand around the glass a few times but never picked it up.

"You looked at me," I said, "and a voice in your head told you I'd hire on to kill your wife."

"I know it sounds crazy."

"Here's something crazier," I said. "I'll do it."

I wound up walking all the way home.

One of the car services had brought him, and he used a cell phone to call for a pickup. Five minutes, he told me, and did I want him to drop me off somewhere? I gave him a look, and I guess he realized that wasn't such a good idea.

I could have told him that coming and going by car service wasn't such a good idea either. He was shaping up to be a curious combination of super cautious and nonchalant, starting out at separate tables and winding up sharing a cab. I decided he had enough to remember, and left him to pay the check.

I'd figured on a bus down Second Avenue. I could transfer to another bus across Fourteenth Street, or I could get off at Seventeenth and walk west for half a mile. But I reached the sidewalk just in time to see my bus pull away, and I decided it was a nice afternoon and I could walk through the park and then catch a bus the rest of the way. Or a subway, whatever.

But I didn't. I left the park at its southwest corner, Fifty-ninth and Central Park West, and remembered there was a good place for smoothies on the west side of Eighth Avenue somewhere around Fiftieth Street. It was actually between Forty-eighth and Forty-ninth, and I ordered their Protein Bonanza with an extra shot of wheat grass.

Figured I could afford it. Two hundred dollars for sitting at a table for half an hour. That would pay for a lot of wheat grass.

Pay for some cabs, too, but at that hour it was nicer to walk than be stuck in traffic. I was halfway home and might as well walk the rest of the way.

Might give my mind a chance to work a few things out.

Where I live there's a bathroom down the hall, with everybody on the floor sharing it. Aside from the toilet, I don't use it much, as I'd rather shower at the gym.

There's a sink in my room, with a mirror over it, and when I got home I checked the mirror to see if I needed a shave. I didn't, but I stood there anyway, studying the face in the mirror.

I tried to see it with his eyes. What was it that looked like a killer? The eyes? The mouth? The set of the jaw? Or just the way they all went together?

How could he have sensed what I hadn't known myself?

Before I left him at the table, we talked about money.

"It's not enough," I told him.

I said it sounded cut-rate. Seventy-five thousand, like he knew the price ought to be a hundred and was angling for a bargain. When he denied this, I asked him how he'd come up with the number.

He said it was the most cash he could put his hands on without leaving a trail.

"I like round numbers," I said, which wasn't true but I figured it sounded reasonable. We kicked it around, and I decided I could do it for his price, but of course it would all have to be in advance.

He'd thought half in advance, half on completion. Wasn't that how these things were generally done?

"Think it through," I suggested. "Do you really want to have to get money to me when the police have you in their sights? I know I won't be up for another coffee shop rendezvous. Once the job's done, I'll go somewhere for a couple of weeks, and when I get back I'll switch to another gym. Any luck at all we'll never set eyes on each other again."

"If I pay you the whole sum in advance—"

"If you don't," I said, "we can forget the whole thing."

"I see your point. But what recourse would I have if—"

"If what? If I didn't do what I said I'd do?"

"Well?"

"Think it through," I said once again. "Do you really think I'm a person who's about to leave loose ends?"

That was Friday afternoon. Over the weekend I went to a movie—nothing special—and Tuesday evening I met my chess buddy at the club on Sullivan Street. We played three games and he won them all, and at dinner afterward he told me about the game he'd played on Thursday.

"She offered two guys draws," he said, "and they both accepted. It looked to me as though one of them had a winning position, but some things are hard to turn down."

Tell me about it, I thought.

"I opened Ruy Lopez, and we just pushed the pieces around, and all of a sudden I was a pawn down, and the next thing I knew she was killing me with a queen-side attack. She got my rook for one of her knights, and that was enough of that. I tipped my king over and she thanked me for a good game, which was generous of her, because a good game was way more than I gave her."

"I wouldn't have done any better."

"Oh, I don't know. Maybe you'd have displayed hitherto undisclosed brilliance and wiped her off the board. But probably not." He sighed. "I'll say this. She's got a really great pair of tits for a chess player."

That was Tuesday. Two days later I caught a glimpse of Tillman at the gym. He was working out with Troy, and I avoided catching his eye, not wanting to spark a conversation. The next day he was on his own and this time I made a point of catching his eye, and he frowned and shook his head.

I nodded toward the restrooms, and walked across the floor to enter one of them. I closed the door and stood next to it, and a few minutes later someone tried it and found it locked, and then I heard him say, "Monday morning."

I said, just as softly, "It's locker number three-eleven."

"I know."

"And the combination is all ones. Eleven-eleven."

"I remember."

I waited until I heard his footsteps. Then I got out of there and settled in on the leg press machine.

Sunday I got in an early workout, then went over to Penn Station and spent a little over an hour on a train. I got off and walked around and caught another train back to the city.

Kind of a nothing day. I might as well have stayed home.

They have two kinds of lockers at the gym. Most of them are first-come-first-served, available free of charge to all members. They have combination locks built in, and you set the combination before you lock up. At closing time one of the employees throws a switch to unlock all the lockers, and anything left in them goes straight to Lost and Found.

The other lockers, and there's only one wall of them, are smaller, and they're not free. You can rent one for fifty dollars a month. You set the combination, same as with the public lockers, but you're the only one who gets to open it, and you can keep your gear there permanently. I've had #311 for almost as long as I've been a member, and Monday morning I went to it and unlocked it, using the same four-digit combination I'd been using all that time.

Nothing much in there. Fingerless gloves, a spare pair of sneakers. A pair of shorts, a singlet.

I reset the combination to 1-1-1-1 and locked up, went upstairs and got to work on the lat machine. Did a set, upped the weight, did another set, added some more weight, and did a third set to failure. Felt the effects of it, and it was a good feeling.

It was Monday, so that meant he was working with Troy. When I caught his eye all I did was nod, and all he did was nod back, and that was enough. I climbed a flight of stairs and picked out a treadmill.

I stayed on it longer than I usually do. What I do, I synchronize my steps with my breathing, and I count breaths. That's not as OCD as it sounds, because I don't care about the numbers, and when I lose track of the count I just start over. The point is to give my mind something to do while I'm running.

He was gone by the time I was done, and my shorts and top were soaking. I went downstairs and put in 1-1-1-1 and opened my locker. It was as I left it, except for the addition of a fanny pack. The brand was Everest, and I resisted the urge to open it and see what it held.

I reset the combination to the four digits I've always used. Locked up. Had my shower, dried off, got dressed. Fastened the fanny pack around my waist, let my shirt hang down over it.

I stopped for a meal on my way home. I used the restroom, and that gave me another opportunity to resist the urge to check the contents of the fanny pack. I was getting so good at resisting that particular urge that once I was back in my room I had to force myself to work the zipper and make like Little Jack Horner.

Six plain white envelopes, bulging, their flaps fastened. More portraits of Benjamin Franklin, along with a smaller number of General

Grant, all used and out of sequence. I counted, and it was all there. $75,000.

And, in one of the envelopes, a key. A house key, from the look of it, but with no manufacturer's name on it, which suggested that it was a duplicate made by a street-front locksmith. Made recently, judging by how bright it was.

Taped to one side of it was a thin strip of plain paper with an address hand-lettered on it: 454 Witherspoon Place.

I added the key to my key ring, but not before I'd removed the strip of paper, rolled it into a little ball, and flipped it into the trash.

Looked again at the stack of bills.

I won't say it took my breath away, but it got my attention. *Now it's real,* a little voice said, but that was ridiculous. It was no more or less real than it had been before. The only difference was that now I had to figure out what to do with the money.

That was August first, a Monday. On Wednesday the tenth he'd be off to Las Vegas.

My gym's one of a chain, and a few months back they'd opened a new branch on Twenty-third Street, no more than a block or two farther from my place than the one at Twelfth and Greenwich. I went there on Thursday, and I didn't even need a guest pass. The girl on the desk scanned the membership fob that lives on my keychain, and it was the same as swiping in at my home gym.

The configuration on the exercise floors was different, of course, although they had basically the same equipment. I was used to running through my routine in a particular sequence, and I changed things up a little to fit their layout.

That wasn't necessarily a bad thing, because you want to switch things around now and then to give your muscles something to think about. I went to Twenty-third Street again on Friday, and did my bench presses on an inclined bench instead of a flat one. I did this because the flat bench stations were a flight of stairs away from where I happened to be, but I liked the way it felt to do the inclines, liked the way it worked the upper part of the pecs.

Saturday I was back at Greenwich and Twelfth. Sunday too. Monday morning I wasn't sure where I was going until I'd walked to Seventh Avenue and had to pick a direction. I turned left, which was north, and walked up to Twenty-third Street.

Back in my room, I unzipped the fanny pack and took another look at the money. I'd gotten rid of the envelopes, but hadn't been able to think of a better home for the cash than the container it had come in, or a better place for the fanny pack itself than the bottom dresser drawer.

Not terribly secure. Well, I'd think of something.

Around noon I rode the subway to Penn Station. The train I took goes all the way to Hackettstown, but they call it the Morristown Line, because there's another train that starts out on a different route and also winds up in Hackettstown. They call that one the Montclair-Boonton Line.

There's a town where both lines merge and head for Hackettstown, but that was three stops past where I'd be getting off. In, duh, Morristown.

I wasn't paying any attention, so I can't swear the train left on time or arrived on time, but I didn't see a lot of people checking their watches and looking upset, so I guess we were more or less on schedule.

I checked out the cars in the train station lot and spotted a blue Kia squareback that looked familiar. The house on Witherspoon Place was within a mile of the station, an easy fifteen-minute walk, and if he walked to and from the station every morning he could put in less time on the elliptical trainer, but people are funny that way. My gym has an elevator, mainly for the Salvadoran women who have to move carts full of towels from one floor to another, but a lot of the clients use it, too. They'll let it lift them up a couple of flights, then hop onto the StairMaster and work up a sweat.

Funny.

I walked to his house, remembering the route from eight days ago when I'd taken the same train ride and gotten off at the same station. That was before I'd collected the money, so I hadn't had a shiny brass key to his front door, but I'd learned his address by looking him up online, and Google Maps had shown me how to get there.

Well, the house was still there. Good-sized two-story house. Driveway running alongside it on the right, with a detached two-car garage in back. On Sunday the garage door had been raised, and I'd seen the Kia and a big Lexus SUV. Today it was closed.

I stood and watched the house for a while, and might have seen something if there'd been something to see, but there wasn't. I walked the length of the driveway. You needed a remote control to raise the garage door, but there was a people-sized door on the side of the garage, and I went and tried it.

It was locked, and what was the point of locking a door with a window? Break the glass and you're in.

Seemed more trouble than it was worth. I did try the key he'd given me, on the off-chance that it would open the garage, but didn't really expect it to work. The garage was dark inside, but there was enough light so that I could see that the SUV was there and the little square-back wasn't. That suggested two things: the car at the station was probably his, and she was probably home.

I put the key back in my pocket, walked around to the front of the house, and rang the doorbell.

*   *   *

A little while later I was back at the train station. The blue Kia was where I'd last seen it, and I figured there was even less chance he'd left it unlocked than that his house key would fit his garage door, but I checked anyway. No luck.

Locked cars are easy enough to open, but you need a Slim-Jim, and I didn't have one. I decided that was probably just as well, as it was a warm day and the Kia was parked in the sun, and who knew how long a wait I'd have? Ten minutes was more time that I really wanted to spend in a hot car, and it might be two or three hours before he showed up.

As it turned out, it was more like forty-five minutes.

I spent the time on a bench up on the platform, and I had the bench and most of the platform to myself, as there weren't all that many people waiting to board the train from Morristown to Hackettstown. The platform would fill up when a train came in and some homebound commuters got off, and then they would abandon me and head for the stairs.

This happened three times while I was on my bench, once a few minutes after I settled in, a second time twenty minutes later, and again at twenty minutes past six. Each time I scanned the passengers departing the train, and the third time was the charm. There he was, dressed in khakis and a seersucker blazer, and paying more attention to his cell phone than to where he was going.

I don't think he'd have spotted me anyway. I stayed where I was and waited until he was a couple of steps past me before getting to my feet. I stayed just behind him, followed him down the stairs and through the station to the parking lot, where he had to look around before he spotted the Kia, as if he'd forgotten where he parked it. He headed for it, and I approached it from a slightly different angle, and got there just as he was keying the lock.

I put a hand on his shoulder, and he was shocked that someone was touching him, shocked again when he saw who it was.

"Easy," I said. "We've got to talk."

"What's the matter? Jesus, you didn't do it already, did you? You're supposed to wait until I'm in Vegas."

"I didn't do anything," I said.

"Well, that's a relief. But—"

I told him to get in the car, and to open the passenger door for me. I walked around the car, got in, and we both fastened our seatbelts.

I said, "We've got to talk, and I don't want to do it here. I was checking, and no one paid any attention to the two of us, but we don't want to risk being spotted together. Is there a mall nearby?"

"A mall?"

"Like a shopping mall. Some place with parking for a couple of thousand cars."

I had a place picked out, but managed to get him to think of it himself, and he drove to it. On the way he wanted to know what the problem was, and I slowed the conversation by turning around to make sure no one was following us.

Then I said, "Remember that guy? Over in Danville?"

"I don't even know where that is."

"Danville, a couple of towns over. Where that nut job killed the woman in the garden apartment."

"*Den*ville," he said, coming down hard on the first syllable. "Not Danville. Denville."

And he rolled his eyes. I really liked that. Genius couldn't remember where he parked his car that morning, but I'm the asshole for screwing up the name of some Jersey shithole with two stop signs.

"My mistake. I keep thinking Danville because of the song."

He didn't ask what song, meaning either he knew or he didn't care.

Then I guess he got past the Denville/Danville snag and wanted to know what had happened. "Shit," he said. "What did they do, catch the guy?"

"Is that what you heard?"

"Huh? I didn't hear anything, for Christ's sake. You're the one who brought him up."

"As far as I know," I said, "he's still at large."

"Well, that's good. For us, I mean."

"You think?"

"Well, isn't it? If he's still on the loose, there's a good chance they'll think he's to blame when Nerissa gets what's coming to her. Isn't that what we talked about?"

"This right here is perfect," I said, pointing. "And they've got one of those twelve-screen movie houses at the far end, and their lot's pretty close to empty at this hour. Park there, why don't you? But, you know, not too close to the entrance."

Driving there.

"So what did he do?"

"Who?"

"The nut job. Who else have we been talking about?"

"There's a good spot," I said.

"He did it again," he said. "That's got to be it. Another housewife? Still in Denville?"

He put it in park, cut the ignition.

I said, "Denville? I thought it was Danville."

Sweet.

A few minutes later I said, "Here's the thing. You came at me from absolutely out of nowhere. 'Hey, you, kill my wife.' Something you sensed, and I'll never know how you sensed it, but one way or another you knew that A—I could do it and B—I *would* do it.

"Now how in the hell could you know something like that, when I didn't know it myself? And could it possibly be true?

"I didn't see how it could. I'd never had any thoughts in that direction. But now you got me thinking, and one day the thought got to me. I started getting excited. Let the fantasy run through my head, and couldn't believe my own reaction.

"Next thing I know, I'm checking Craig's List, looking for someone selling something. It could have been anywhere, but maybe I wanted to have the dress rehearsal close to where the real thing would go down. I don't remember thinking that, but it's possible I had it in mind. What do you think?"

He didn't answer.

"Well, whatever. This was Thursday, the day after you got me to spot you on the bench press. I made a few calls, and one of them was to a woman who was looking to sell a free-standing air conditioner. Instead of having to mount it in a window or cut a hole in the wall, you just stand it up on the floor and plug it in. Anyway, she had one, and she said it worked fine, but the apartment complex was putting in through-the-wall units for everybody, so she thought she'd put Old Faithful up for sale.

"She said she lived in Denville, and when I said I'd be coming by train she offered to pick me up. She was so nice about it that I thought, well, I'm not gonna be able to do this, so I'll just go and look at the unit and tell her it won't really work for me, and the next time I see you I'll tell you to shit in your hat, or do your own killing, or whatever.

"So I got on the train, and realized that I didn't have to see her in person to tell her I didn't want her air conditioner. I could have called back and found something to say, or saved the phone call and just failed to show up. But I was on the train, and I knew I wanted to do it.

"Perfectly nice woman, a little bit Chatty Cathy, but pleasant.

Pretty in a bland way, nothing special. She picked me up at the station and drove me a couple of miles to her apartment development, and I kept thinking we'd run into somebody on the way, some witness, or there'd be somebody at her apartment, and that would be the end of that, and I might not buy her air conditioner but she'd still have a pulse when I got back on my train and went home.

"Nobody in the parking lot, nobody in the halls, nobody in her apartment. And once we're inside and the door's shut, there's no fucking way to keep the rest of it from unfolding. Be easier to stop a train.

"She demonstrated how the unit worked, and how cold the air was that came out of it, and I said, 'I'm really sorry about this.' She was trying to figure out what I meant when I hit her.

"And then you know, I did what I did."

I stopped there, and let myself remember the way it had felt. I'd been two people at once, one of them doing what I did, the other observing. I suppose it was the observer half who made sure I used a condom, made sure I left no prints or obvious trace evidence. Still, I did wind up walking all the way back to the train station. Anyone could have seen me, but evidently no one did.

"Just dumb luck," I said now. "I had a long wait for the train, and I kept listening for sirens and waiting for the long arm of the law to take me by the shoulder, but by the time my train came I knew none of that was going to happen. I'd killed a woman for no reason at all, and if they hadn't gotten me right away they weren't going to get me at all. Even if I'd left DNA behind, they couldn't match it to me unless I came up on their radar.

"Train pulled out of Denville and passed through Mount Tabor and Morris Plains and then Morristown. I knew that's where you and Nerissa lived, I'd checked you out before I got to Craig's List. And I damn well knew it was Denville and not Danville. First time I said it wrong it was to avoid sounding too familiar with the place, because I didn't want you guessing I'd been there, but after that it just got to be fun. Jerking on your chain, you know?"

No response from him.

I said, "Anyway, I'd answered part of my question. Could I do something like this? Well, yes, I could. That was pretty well established, in that I'd just done it.

"And I knew the answer to the second part, too. Would I do it—do it for you, do it to your wife, and do it to earn seventy-five thousand dollars?

"You know, it took me a little time to be sure of my answer. Because I can't say I didn't get any pleasure out of what I did in Denville. I can't explain it, but there was something exciting about it. Afterward it left me feeling empty, and sorry I'd done it. I don't know whether or not to call it remorse, but there's no question I felt a certain amount of regret.

"Would I want to do it again? I gather that's what happens with people who make a habit of this sort of thing. They get something out of it that makes them do it again. And again, and again. I had to live with the whole thing for a while before I could rule it out, but the days passed and I knew I wasn't going to find some other innocent like the Denville girl, and I wasn't going after Nerissa Tillman, either.

"But I kind of wanted the money. I hadn't thought about large sums of money before, anymore than I'd thought about killing anybody, but the idea got in my head and I decided I wanted it, even if I didn't know what I wanted it for. I knew I didn't want to kill your wife, but I thought maybe I should go ahead and do it anyway, just because I wanted the money.

"Except I'd get caught.

"I mean, face it, man. No matter how much I made it look like the Denville killing, no matter how they might want to believe both acts were the work of the same man, they just had to look long and hard at you, you know? You're the husband, you had a reason to want her dead, and they always look first and longest and hardest at the husband, because he almost always either did it or hired it done.

"And you'd crack like a fucking egg.

"You would, you know. They'd want to talk to you, and you'd know you ought to lawyer up right away, but how would that look? A man's wife's dead, the probable victim of a serial killer, and a couple of sympathetic cops come to talk to him, and the first words out of his mouth are 'I want a lawyer.' Is that the way an innocent man would react?

"So you wouldn't do that, not right away. You'd start out all earnest and cooperative, and by the time you realized your mistake you'd have told them more than you meant to. If nothing else, they'd come out of that interview room knowing you were their guy, and all they had to do was find out who you'd hired.

"And, one way or another, you'd tell them. 'Mr. Tillman, we figure you just wanted him to scare her a little. That was your deal, and it was just bad luck that you picked a homicidal maniac, or maybe she fought back and he lost control, but he's the one who did the killing and he's the one we want, and if you cooperate and come up with a name—' A couple of smart cops who do this sort of thing all the time, and you're the textbook definition of an amateur, and do you want to tell me you'd have been able to hold out? Go ahead, let's hear you say it."

Not a word.

"Right," I said. "That's what I figured. With you to point me out, they wouldn't waste any time picking me up. And they'd probably have me, too, once they knew who to look for, but I could stop all that by not getting picked up in the first place, and that meant not doing the job.

"But I still wanted the money. It was pulling at me, the same way the idea of killing someone had pulled at me early on.

"Remember why you balked at paying me the full sum in front?

Because that way you wouldn't have any leverage. Because what was to stop me from taking your money and walking off with it?

"Remember what I said? Like, am I the sort of person who's gonna leave a loose end?

"You know what I did this afternoon? After I got off the train, and before I grabbed you by the shoulder? I took a walk out to your house on Witherspoon Place. I was thinking about waiting for you in the garage, but I didn't want to smash a window, and then I thought about this mall and its nice big parking lot and I made my choice.

"But before I came back to the station I rang your doorbell.

"Because aside from that picture I'd never really laid eyes on your wife, and I wanted to meet her. So I rang the bell and she came to the door. She was wearing jeans and a blouse, sandals on her feet, and she's a fine-looking woman, but I guess you know that. You may not care, the way the marriage has broken down, but you're still aware of it, right?

"We talked through the screen door. I said something about some people in the area reporting a problem with cable reception, and she said hers was working fine, and I said I was sorry to have bothered her.

"And I turned around and walked back to the train station to wait for you. And take care of a loose end.

"Jesus, man, even if I did the fucking job, even if I killed your wife and ran her through a fucking woodchipper, you're still a loose end. You're the loosest end there is. Go on, let me hear you deny it."

But he didn't say anything. And, really, how could he? Right after he'd put the car in park I'd got hold of him by the throat, and by the time he realized what was happening, well, it had pretty much happened. And we were still parked in the same spot, and all this time I'd been having a conversation with a dead man.

Better than having him interrupting all the time, going all Denville-Danville on me.

The parking area around the cinema was starting to fill up, as it got closer to showtime, but we didn't have any next-door neighbors yet. Even so it was time I got out of there. I could switch places with him, start the engine and get myself a little closer to the train station before we parted company. But I checked the map app on my phone, and saw that I could walk the whole distance in under an hour.

It seemed simpler that way. I'd been careful what I touched in the car, and wiped off any surfaces my fingers might have brushed, and took a moment to position him so that he looked like a man sitting behind the wheel and waiting for his wife to return to their car.

It wasn't a bad walk. Cooler now, with the sun down. Quiet tree-lined suburban streets, not much in the way of auto traffic, and the only pedestrians were out walking their dogs.

It had been satisfying, killing him. The Denville killing had had sex mixed in, and you'd think that would make it better, but I actually liked it better this way. I'd made money, and I'd tied off a loose end, and the body I left behind was somebody I didn't like very much. Somebody I actually disliked, come right down to it.

Wondered if this was something I'd do again. Impossible to say, really. Couldn't rule it in, couldn't rule it out.

A long walk, clear back to the train station. But what I did, same as I'll do on the treadmill, I synched my breathing to my steps and counted breaths. Something for my mind to do, you know?

Worked just fine.

Resume Speed

In Galbraith, the Trailways bus station was a single room with a pitched ceiling, where a clerk dispensed hunting and fishing licenses and tobacco products in addition to bus tickets. There was no place to sit, so he waited outside, feeling exposed. As soon as his coach pulled up, he walked to the curb to board it, his bag in one hand, his ticket in the other. The bus was no more than a third full, and he found an empty pair of seats in the rear. He hoisted his bag into the overhead rack, dropped into the window seat, and let out a breath he hadn't even realized he'd been holding.

And then there was a small series of similar exhalations, of knots dissolving and tensions giving way. When the driver closed the doors and pulled away from the curb. When a sign announced the town line, and another said *Resume Speed*.

Minnie Pearl's home town, he thought. Years since he'd recalled the line. Years since he'd even thought of Minnie Pearl.

Another town, and another, and if they had *Resume Speed* signs of their own, he never noticed them. And, finally, the state line—and he drew a deep breath and let it out, and looked down at his hands, folded neatly in his lap.

Thoughts came, pointless thoughts, questions without answers. He blinked them away and breathed them away, and the bus stopped, and somebody got off and somebody got on, and the seat beside him remained empty, and the bus started up again. And, with or without a sign to prompt it, resumed speed.

His eyes closed. He slept.

When he opened his eyes he was in a town and the bus had stopped moving. Were they at a bus stop? No, they were idling at a traffic light, waiting for it to turn. He looked out the window, and two doors up the street was a diner. Neon spelled out its name: *Kalamata*.

And there was a hand-lettered sign in the window. He squinted at it and couldn't swear what it said, but he had a fair idea.

And it felt like the right size town, big enough to have a traffic light, and far enough down the line from where he'd boarded. When they reached the station, he'd get off.

Unless they'd already stopped at whatever passed for a bus station in whatever town this was. He could have slept through it. Well, there'd be another town, and another diner. His ticket was good clear through to Spokane. If it stopped here he'd get off, and if it didn't he'd ride on, and either way it made no never mind.

Then the bus braked again, and he heard the driver say "Cross Creek," which was evidently the name of where they were. He'd never heard of Cross Creek, but it pretty much had to be in Montana, and on balance it made a more likely name for the town than Kalamata.

The seat next to his was still empty, so there was no one to disturb as he got to his feet and retrieved his carry-on from the overhead. When he reached the driver, the fellow told him they were just stopping to load and unload passengers. If he wanted a smoke break, he'd best wait until they got to Billings.

"I'm gonna leave you here," he told the man.

"Thought you was ticketed clear to Spokane."

"Somebody here I been meaning to see," he said. "Spokane can wait."

"Spokane ain't going nowhere," the driver agreed. "That all you got or do I need to open up the luggage?"

He shook his head. "Just this."

"Like the song." He must have looked puzzled. "You know. *Traveling Light.*"

"Always," he said.

He hadn't been counting the blocks, but he figured he couldn't be more than half a mile from the diner. A straight shot back the way he'd come. The bus hadn't turned off, just pulled up in front of the station—which happened to house a lunch counter of its own. He thought about stopping for something, maybe a grilled cheese sandwich, maybe a side of fries. But what kind of fool has a meal on his way to a restaurant?

Kalamata. Could be a Japanese tourist trying to say Calamity. He thought of Calamity Jane, who'd hung out a ways east of here, in Deadwood, if he remembered correctly. Pretty sure it was Deadwood. Although it could be that she'd gotten around some, which you'd have to expect from a woman with Calamity for a name.

His watch said 3:18, but maybe it was an hour earlier, maybe they'd crossed into a different time zone. So it was a little after three or a little after two, which amounted to the same thing in restaurant time. Past lunch and a ways to go until dinner, which made it down time, which was how he wanted it.

One foot in front of the other, and maybe it was a little more than half a mile, but it had to be there, and sure enough it was. *Kalamata,* all in neon. And the hand-lettered sign, black block caps on a sheet of ruled paper torn from a spiral-bound notebook.

EXPERIENCED
FRY COOK
WANTED

He opened the door, walked in. Booths, tables, a counter along the wall on the right. Checkerboard tiles on the floor. Formica counter and table tops. Pennants on the wall—Cross Creek High, Montana State University. Two women sat over coffee at a booth in the back, smoke from their cigarettes drifting toward the ceiling. He'd smelled smoke in the air right away, against an overlay of cooking smells.

Pretty typical, really.

The Fry Cook sign was fastened to the inside of the door with clear tape, and he removed it, tape and all, and carried it to the man planted behind the counter. Stocky, jowly, black hair, thick moustache. Dark eyes that said they'd seen it all.

He handed the sign across the counter. "You can put this away," he said. "I'm your man."

The eyebrows went up a half inch. "Just get to town?"

"Does it show? Oh, this." He set his bag on a stool. "Just got off the bus."

"Where you worked?"

"Just about everywhere, one time or another. Some white-tablecloth joints, but mostly short order. I could give you references."

"What for? Work a counter and a griddle, a man can do it or he can't. Grab that apron off the hook there, then come on back and make me an omelet."

"What kind?"

"What kind you like?"

"For myself, I tend to keep it simple. Just cheese."

"You get a choice. Swiss, cheddar, feta."

"I like feta on a salad," he said, "but my first choice for an omelet is Swiss."

"So make a Swiss cheese omelet. We do three eggs, serve toast with it. White or whole wheat?"

"Whole wheat."

"And a side of fries."

"Got it," he said.

He got to work. He thought, feta cheese in the middle of Montana, and the guy looked like a Greek to begin with, so it wasn't a Japanese trying to say Calamity Jane, it was some kind of Greek word, and hadn't he heard it before?

Right.

He put the omelet on a plate, added the fries, set it on the counter. He'd already buttered the two slices of toast and put them on a smaller plate.

"Why give it to me?"

"I thought you might want to taste it, see if it's okay."

"No eggs for me, no fried food either. Doctor's a pain in my ass. No, I don't need to taste it, I watched you make it, I know what it's gonna taste like. No, it's for you. Just off a bus, you gotta be hungry, unless you went and made a mistake and ate at the bus station."

"I didn't."

"Good, 'cause you'd be taking your life in your hands. Sit down, dig in. You want coffee? No, stay there, I'll get it for you."

He started eating, and forced himself not to wolf his food. This was breakfast and lunch, his first meal since an early dinner the previous evening, and he always liked his own cooking.

Halfway through, he paused for a moment and said, "Olives."

"How's that?"

"Kalamata," he said. "Rang a bell and I couldn't think what, but it's olives, isn't it? A fancy kind of olives."

The man smiled. "Big purple bastards. When I got 'em in stock, we put three in the Greek salad. Otherwise it's black olives from the Food Barn. It's not like anybody around here knows the difference. My father named the place, and it's not for the olives. It's a city in Greece, and he got the hell out as soon as he could. So you got to wonder why he stuck the name on the restaurant."

"You've never been there."

"And never will. If I was gonna fly somewhere, well, I wouldn't mind seeing Paris. But it'd be a miracle if I ever got out of Montana. It's not bad here, Cross Creek."

"It seems nice."

"And that leads to my question, which is will you stick around a while? Because you know what you're doing and I could for sure use you, but if you're just saving up for your next bus ticket, you know, it's not doing me much good if you take off just about the time you get the hang of how we do it here. You know what I'm saying?"

He nodded. "I'm not planning to go anywhere."

"All your life, you dreamed of making a home for yourself in Cross Creek, Montana."

"I never heard of it until I got off the bus," he said. "Anyway, I don't have any dreams."

"No?"

"Maybe once," he said, "but not in years. What I've learned, one place is as good as the next."

"You know that, you know plenty."

"I don't need much. A job where I get to eat my own cooking, a change of clothes, a place to sleep."

"You didn't get a room yet."

"No, not without having a job first."

"Well, you got a job. I been close to two months now since I let the last guy go. He was okay behind the stick, nothing special, but he missed too many days. And some mornings he came in with the shakes, and you knew right away what was making him miss those days. That a problem of yours?"

"No. But if it was, I'd probably say it wasn't."

"Yeah, soon as I asked I wondered why I bothered. You got a name?"

"Bill," he said. "Last name's Thompson."

"Good solid American name. Mine's Andy Page."

"Another solid American name."

"Well, I can say it's the name I was born with, but it wasn't Page until my father got off the boat. You're hired, Bill. Now let's figure out hours and money."

That didn't take long. They came quickly to terms and shook hands on it.

"So you got a job," Andy said. "You want another cup of coffee? Piece of pie? The pecan's real good."

"Not now, thanks."

"No, what you want is to get a room and settle in. There's a hotel a block the other side of the Trailways that's not too bad. Or there's a couple of places that rent rooms."

"I passed a place about two blocks back."

"Other side of Main? Big yellow house, got a hairdresser on the ground floor? That's Mrs. Minnick, and if she had a sign in the window, you want to get there before she takes it down. Her place is decent and she keeps it clean, and if you're a good tenant—"

"I'm a good tenant."

"Yeah, I expect you are. Tell her you're my new fry cook. I think you'll like it there."

"I think I'll like it here."

"Well, I hope you do, Bill. I hope you do. Go ahead, get your room, get settled. Then come in tomorrow morning and you can start cooking some breakfasts."

*   *   *

There were things Andy had his own way of doing, but it was always like that, and it wasn't as though Bill Thompson was wedded to his own routine. He got the hang of it right away, and he remembered things. You didn't have to tell him twice.

And he was as much at home behind the counter as he was on the grill, and had a nice easy way with the customers. Not too easy, because an excess of familiarity could put people off. Especially the women, and Kalamata was a place where a woman by herself was comfortable sitting at the counter, and some of them liked to be flirted with and some didn't, and you needed to be able to size them up and read the signals they gave off. You didn't hit on them, that wasn't part of the deal under any circumstances, but some would think you were standoffish if you didn't flirt a little, and others would think you were overstepping boundaries if you did, and it wasn't a logic problem, you couldn't sit down and work it out with pencil and paper. You needed the right instincts, and he had them.

His room at Gerda Minnick's was as nice as any he could recall. Some years back he'd had a house of his own, a living room and kitchen in front, two bedrooms in back, on an eighth of an acre on the edge of town, and what town was it? He could picture the house, he could have drawn the floor plan, but he had to think to come up with Fort Smith, Arkansas. Little scrubby lawn, little spindly birch tree in the middle of it, and the bank that foreclosed on the house had been happy to rent it to him for less than he generally had to pay for a furnished room. The agent told him how the lease included an option to buy the property at the end of the year, and explained how it would be to his advantage to do so, and he considered it off and on. It was okay, it had to be a step up to have a whole house all to yourself, but the construction cut all the corners and the basement was damp, and what did a fry cook want with a home kitchen?

Moot point, as he'd left the city and the state with five months left to go on his lease.

At Mrs. Minnick's he had two flights of carpeted stairs to climb, and he shared the bathroom down the hall with another tenant, but the room itself was large and well-proportioned and the furniture was sound and serviceable and there were windows looking north and west.

There were rules. There was a TV in the parlor, but if he wanted to bring in a set of his own, he'd have to shut it off, or at least mute it, between the hours of eleven in the evening and 7:30 in the morning. No radio playing during those hours, either, and no loud music any time of the day or night. No running the shower between midnight and six. No guests, same sex or opposite, in the rooms. No smoking anywhere in the house. Spirits were not prohibited, but drunkenness was.

That was all fine with him.

She quoted him a price. "Or you could pay by the month for four times the weekly rate. That'll save you a few dollars every month, except in February it won't save you a nickel."

Was he supposed to laugh? He couldn't tell, she delivered the line in the same toneless tone that she'd told him when he could and couldn't take a shower. He thought of saying something about Leap Year and decided against it.

There was a week of April left. He handed over a week's rent, said he might switch to a monthly basis on the first of May.

He unpacked his bag, put his clothes in the dresser drawers. There was a lace doily on top of the dresser, positioned to cover the scar where someone's forbidden cigarette had burned itself out.

The only surprise to come out of his bag was his drinking glass, a cylindrical tumbler with six marks along the side to indicate volume from one to six ounces. He couldn't say when it had come into his possession. He hadn't bought it and he rather doubted anyone had, not as a drinking glass, because he rather thought it had started life as a jelly glass; whoever had used the last of the jelly had evidently decided the container was too useful to discard. And he'd evidently made much the same decision himself, finding room for it when he'd hastened to stuff a few things into his bag.

He put the glass on the doily, then sat at the window until the sky began to darken. He walked down the hall, towel and dopp kit in hand, showered, shaved, made sure to leave the tub and the sink as spotless as he'd found them. He returned to his room, found a place for his shaving gear, propped his toothbrush in the six-ounce drinking glass, and hung the towel Mrs. Minnick provided on the bar where he'd found it, and picked out a T-shirt to sleep in.

When he'd filled his suitcase that morning, he'd fastened a money belt around his waist, underneath his clothes. He'd taken it off to shower, put it on again after he'd dried off. It held all his cash, except for a couple of hundred dollars in his wallet. Where to stash it? He looked around, decided it could wait until morning.

He got in bed, arranged the pillow the way he liked it. Closed his eyes, felt sleep moving in on him, took just the briefest moment to think about where he was. He'd done this before, he thought, and he could do it again. Hell, he *was* doing it again.

His life in Cross Creek became a life of regular habits. Six days a week, he worked a full shift at the diner, and the hardest part was figuring out what to do with himself on his days off. If the weather was good he might go for a long walk, might take in a movie. On rainy days there was no reason to leave the house, and barely reason to leave his room.

Once, maybe twice a week, after his shift at Kalamata was done, he'd stop in the downstairs sitting room and pass an hour in front of the television set. The two top-floor tenants were almost always there, one an elderly man who wore plaid shirts and got them buttoned wrong more often than not, the other a retired schoolteacher who always had a book with her to read during the commercials. Mrs. Minnick watched two shows every evening, the network news and *Jeopardy*, and disappeared for the night after the Final Jeopardy segment.

The tenant on his floor, whom he'd barely laid eyes on, never appeared in the TV room. She was morbidly obese and used two canes when she made her way to the bathroom and back. As far as he could tell, that was the only time she ever left her room.

He didn't need much in the way of diversion. The diner kept him busy from seven in the morning to seven at night. That was a long work week, but it wasn't all work, with fallow stretches between breakfast and lunch and again from mid-afternoon until five. And the work was work he was good at, work he enjoyed.

Anything he wanted to eat, he cooked it and ate it. Nothing wrong with that.

He stayed week-to-week at Mrs. Minnick's through May. On the last Thursday in the month, he finished his shift, walked home, and continued past his rooming house and down to the next block, where the sign was a braided rope coiled to spell out *The Stockman*. He went in, took in the familiar smell of a tavern, and walked up to the bar. He ordered a glass of beer and drank it, then looked over the bourbons and bought a pint of Old Crow. The bartender took his money and handed him the bottle in a brown paper sack.

He brought it home and stowed it, still in the sack, in a dresser drawer.

The following day he came straight home from work. He needed a shower, and took one, but decided Thursday's shave could last another day. Back in his room, he opened a window for the breeze and lay down on the bed for half an hour. He almost fell asleep, but didn't, and got up and dressed.

How, he wondered, did they come up with Old Crow as a name for a brand of whiskey? The label, with its illustration of a dapper black bird, held no clue. He decided that Crow, spelled that way or with an E at the end, was very likely the name of the original distiller.

Before uncapping the bottle, he took his toothbrush from the glass and found a place to set it down. He poured precisely two ounces of bourbon and seated himself by the open window. Someone was running a power mower, near enough so that he could smell the fresh-cut grass. He took a moment to enjoy the smell, and then he raised the glass and breathed in the smell of the Old Crow, and enjoyed that, too.

Drank it right down. Liked the taste, liked the burn. It was smooth enough, but there was just enough of a burn to let you know that what you were drinking deserved a measure of respect.

Sat there, looking out the window, listening to the sound of the mower, breathing in the smell of fresh-mown grass.

After maybe five minutes he walked down the hall to the bathroom, where he rinsed and dried the glass. Back in his room, he put it back in its place, set the toothbrush in it. Returned the bottle to the dresser drawer.

The following afternoon he came home, showered, shaved. Drank his two ounces of Old Crow. He had the same ration of whiskey each of the next two days, and on the first of June he paid Gerda Minnick four times the weekly rent.

"So you're month-to-month now," she said.

"It suits me."

She nodded thoughtfully, and came as close as she ever did to a smile. "Well, you're no trouble," she told him.

He'd been wearing the money belt every day, though after a couple of days he'd begun removing it when he went to bed and donning it in the morning. The same night that he paid a month's rent all at once, he stowed the money belt at the back of the bottom drawer.

Partly, he supposed, because he'd seen no sign that anybody went in his room, except on the day when the girl came in to change the bed, leave a clean towel, and run the vacuum. He'd left little traps once or twice, just to see if she opened a drawer, and she hadn't done so.

So wearing the belt seemed an unnecessary precaution, and an increasingly cumbersome one, as the belt was thicker than it had been when he got off the bus. He wasn't earning a fortune working for Andy Page, but his rent—weekly or monthly—was low, and of course his meals were free. He'd bought himself a shirt and a second pair of shoes—he'd left with only the ones on his feet. Aside from that, he'd hardly spent any money at all.

For a couple of days it felt strange to be walking around without that pressure in the small of his back. But he got used to it.

There were magazines in the parlor, and he was leafing through a year-old copy of *Time* when he came across the card you mailed in for a subscription. It was offered with a guarantee; if you didn't like it, you wrote CANCEL across the invoice and mailed it back.

He filled out the card: William M. Thompson, 318 E. Main Street,

Cross Creek MT. He didn't know the zip, but copied it from an address label on another of the magazines.

Mailed it in the morning and forgot about it.

Mail for tenants was stacked on a cherry end table in the vestibule. One evening there was a copy of *Time* on the table, addressed to him. He took it upstairs and turned the pages while he drank his two ounces of Old Crow, then set it on his own bedside table.

A few days later the bill came. He put it with the magazine, and over the next two weeks he received two more issues of *Time*, along with junk mail from another magazine—*Sports Illustrated*—and a few charities, including an organization that provided therapy dogs to wounded veterans.

When his next day off came around, he went to the Cross Creek Public Library. He'd stopped there before, but this time he applied for a library card, and for ID he showed his rent receipt, along with a copy of *Time* and several pieces of mail addressed to him. He thought he'd have to come back in a day or two for the card, but the librarian made it out on the spot.

"I never knew your name," she said, "but I recognize you well enough, Mr. Thompson."

"Oh?"

"From the restaurant. You wouldn't have noticed me, I always sit in a back booth, and I've generally got my face buried in a book."

"Next time," he said, "come sit at the counter."

He found a book to borrow, *Golden Spike*, about the building of the first transcontinental railroad. She checked him out and told him to bring it back for renewal if he didn't finish it in the allotted month. Otherwise there'd be a fine, and it wasn't steep, but why pay a fine if you didn't have to?

He went home, discarded the various pieces of junk mail he'd brought with him, and added his copy of *Time* to the stack in the parlor. He printed CANCEL on the *Time* invoice, mailed it back the following day.

The book was interesting. He'd thought it might be, hadn't just grabbed it off the shelf, but neither had he counted on getting caught up in it. For five nights running he sat down with the book and his two ounces of bourbon, just sipping the whiskey while he followed the story of the building of the Union Pacific Railroad, from the laying of the first rails in Omaha to the sinking of the titular golden spike at Promontory Summit, Utah.

The next day, a few minutes past noon, he was behind the counter at Kalamata when the librarian paused in the doorway. He flashed a welcoming smile, and pointed at a stool.

"Oh," she said. "I always want support for my back. But these stools have backs, don't they? I never noticed that before."

The special, he told her, was goulash. "My own recipe," he said, and she said that in that case she'd have to try it.

It was the diner's busy time, and he had meals to prepare and customers to serve, but they'd had a few exchanges by the time he took away her bowl and brought her coffee. When he set the cup in front of her she said, "Thank you, Mr. Thompson," and he told her to please call him Bill. That gave her the opportunity to tell him she was Carlene Weldon, and to please call her Carlene.

"Carlene," he said.

The next morning was Thursday, his day off. He rose and showered and shaved, although he'd shaved the day before, and left the house with *Golden Spike* under his arm. He'd stayed up late the previous night to finish it.

Carlene was at the front desk, talking on the phone. It gave him a moment to look at her without being himself observed.

Her hair was light brown, cropped close to her head, and in a large city on either coast she might have been taken for a lesbian. But he knew she wasn't.

Her face was heart-shaped, her features regular and unremarkable. Large eyes, a clear pale blue in color. She wore ironed jeans and a red-and-white checked blouse, and her body was neither slender nor plump. No ring on her finger, and no mark where one might recently have been. She looked like what she almost certainly was, a woman in her early thirties whose life offered everything a solitary life could provide.

Each of them, he thought, was just about the last thing the other needed. He was examining that thought, and wondering where it ought to lead, when she replaced the receiver and looked up at him. Her smile reached all the way to her eyes.

"If you liked *Golden Spike*—"

"I did, very much."

"Well, was it railroads generally? Or the history, the role the Union Pacific played in the development of the country? Because either way I could suggest a book or two you might like."

The answer came easily. "The history of it. I got a real sense of the way the country used to be, and the way people saw things."

She knew just the book. "It's set back east, and a number of years before anybody was thinking about transcontinental railroads." It was called *Wedding of the Waters,* and it was about the building of the Erie Canal. He opened the book at random, read a couple of paragraphs, and knew he wanted to read more.

He gave her his library card and she did the paperwork, then invited him to browse. Perhaps he'd find something else he liked. Oh, could he borrow more than one book at a time? She assured him he could. Up to five, she said.

He made a show of browsing, picking the occasional volume from the shelf, turning the pages, putting it back. He figured one book at a time was plenty, given that he'd paid his first visit to the library for the sole purpose of obtaining a library card.

Off to one side, an oak table held four desktop computers, with patrons seated at two of them. A sign explained that computer use was free, but there was a half-hour limit. You could print anything you downloaded, for a fee of 25¢ a page.

He stood there for a moment, then shook his head and turned away. Why spoil a nice day?

She was busy on her own computer when he returned to her desk, but she looked up at his approach. "I think I'll have my hands full with the Erie Canal," he said. "But I do have a question."

"Part of my job description, isn't it? Answering questions."

"What I haven't worked out yet," he said, "is where to eat when I have the day off. I could go back to Andy's, but—"

"But that way it doesn't feel like a day off."

"What it feels like," he said, "is I ought to put on an apron and wash up after myself. I figure one night a week it'd be nice to sit down someplace with a white tablecloth and let somebody wait on me."

She told him about three restaurants, only one of them in Cross Creek. She seemed particularly fond of the Conestoga Inn, located halfway between Cross Creek and Burnham, and he said it sounded really nice.

"But too far to walk to," he said.

"Oh, I'd say. It's twenty miles, or close to. You don't have a car?"

"Or even a license. Last place I lived you could get along fine without a car, and I went and junked the one I had when the transmission quit. My license was out-of-state, and I never bothered trying to renew it, or getting a new one."

She nodded, taking this in.

"What I'm thinking," he said, "is this Conestoga place sounds just right, except for two things. It's too far to walk, and it sounds like way too nice a place for a man to dine alone."

Something else for her to take in.

"So if you'd provide the transportation," he went on, "it'd be my pleasure to provide the dinner. As far as conversation's concerned, I figure that would be our joint responsibility."

When the waiter took their drink order, she asked for a Diet Coke. He said he'd have the same.

When he said something about her name, she said, "I'd have been Carl Jr. if I hadn't been a girl. And they were just positive I'd be a boy. There was this old Indian woman who supposedly always got it right."

"Until you came along."

"And I could have been Carla but my mother came up with Carlene instead. There's a singer, Carlene Carter, and there was a country song, a man singing about a girl from high school. 'Carlene.' You would hear it a lot but you never hear it anymore. In thirty-four years I've never met another Carlene."

"Over the years," he said, "I've run into a fellow named Bill now and then."

"Well, I guess. Your full name's tons more common than my first name. Bill Thompson. Not quite John Smith, but not too far off."

"I could change it to Carlene, but people might look at me funny. Are your parents—?"

She shook her head. "He disappeared when I was in the second grade. We never heard from him, not a word. I couldn't guess where he'd be living, or even *if* he's living. And she died, oh, it's better than eight, close to nine years now. Nine years in November. Do you have any brothers or sisters?"

One of each, but he'd lost touch with both, and did either of them need to be in this conversation?

"No," he said.

"Neither do I. I used to think it would be nice, but they say the only child learns to be self-reliant."

"And are you?"

"Self-reliant?" She thought about it. "I guess so. I seem to be all right at getting along on my own. I got along when my father left and when my mother died, and when my marriage failed."

"You were married."

"I'm divorced longer than I was married. Two years married, three years divorced. That's a strange expression, isn't it? A marriage failing, like a business with too much money going out and not enough coming in. Except you couldn't explain it by bookkeeping. Have you been married?"

He shook his head. "Came close once or twice."

"What I came close to was backing out at the last minute. What the preacher says, if anyone has any objection to the wedding. You know, speak now or forever hold your peace? I was wishing somebody would speak up. My mama never liked him, but she'd have had to rise from the dead to make her objections known. There was really nobody to speak up, there was nobody at all but the minister and his wife and two witnesses who lived next door. I don't know why I'm going on like this, telling you way more than anybody'd want to hear."

"No, I'm interested."

"I'm in the house I grew up in. I never moved out, and when mama died it got to be my house, and he moved in, and two years later he moved out."

"And you're still there."

"And I'm still there. Born in Cross Creek and likely to die in Cross Creek, and sometimes that seems sad, all that road-not-taken business, and other times what it seems is fitting."

"Andy says he wouldn't mind going to Paris, and in the next breath he says he never will."

"Maybe everybody needs a place to never go to. For me it would be London. Did you ever read a book called *84, Charing Cross Road*? It's all letters, from a woman in New York to a bookstore owner in London. I forget what she was, a writer or an editor or something, but she could just as easily have been a librarian."

"And lived in Montana?"

"Anywhere. For twenty years they wrote each other letters, and all she wanted in the world was to go there and visit the store and meet this man, and by the time she finally went, the store was closed and he was dead."

"Another of those happy endings."

"Life's full of them. Anyway, London is the place I'll never go to. What's yours?"

Home, he thought.

What he said was, "Oh, I don't know. Maybe Hawaii."

They didn't talk on the ride home, but it was an easy silence, with no edge to it. She was a careful driver, her eyes on the road, and he passed the time watching her. He ran different lines through his mind, trying to find the right way to express a desire to see where she lived. He couldn't come up with anything that would seem natural. He could just say something, anything, about her house, and give her the opportunity to ask him if he'd like to see the place.

Wondered, sitting there and looking at her, if she was going through the same little dance in the privacy of her own mind. Wanting to invite him home, worried he might decline, worried he might accept.

She had picked him up a couple of hours ago in front of Mrs. Minnick's house, and now she braked to a stop in the same spot. He had the wild notion to invite her in, simply because it was against the rules. What he said was, "Well, this is where I get off."

"I had a really nice time, Bill."

"Did you? I know I did. Maybe we could—"

"Do this again? I'd like that."

"Do you ever go to the movies? I thought maybe dinner and a movie, one of these nights."

"I'd like that," she said, and rested her hand on top of his. Was it a good time to kiss her? Maybe, if they were standing on a doorstep, but not in the front seat of a Ford Escort.

He passed the parlor without looking in and climbed the stairs to his room. He got ready for bed, then realized he hadn't had a drink. He could have had one before she picked him up, but didn't want it on his breath. Besides, he figured they'd each have one at the restaurant, but when she ordered a Diet Coke he'd followed her lead.

The hell with it, his teeth were brushed, he was already in bed. He turned off the light, drifted off.

There was another date, three nights later. He finished his shift, came home for a shower and shave, and this time he had a drink before she picked him up. They ate at one of the Cross Creek restaurants she'd mentioned, and the waitress greeted her by name.

"She was a year behind me in high school. Pregnant at graduation,"

Carlene explained, and frowned. "Like it matters, all these years later, but you never get over high school, do you?"

"I guess not."

She asked about his high school years, what they were like, and the truth was he couldn't remember them all that well. He said, honestly enough, that he supposed those were difficult years for everybody.

"Even when they're not," she said. "I read something, don't ask me where—"

"Probably the library."

"You think? What it said, there was a follow-up study on what the high school experience felt like ten years down the line. And the ordinary kids all said the same thing, how self-conscious they were, how isolated they felt, how they couldn't wait to get to the next stage in their lives. But you know what the cool kids said? The athletes, the class presidents, the beauty queens?"

"What?"

"Exactly the same thing! They looked to be having the time of their lives, and they were just as miserable as the rest of us."

The room was nicely appointed, with a high ceiling and plenty of room between the tables. Framed landscapes on the walls, suspended from the crown molding. But he felt they dished out better food at Andy's diner.

He wouldn't have said so, but she made the observation herself as they walked from the restaurant to the movie house. "They use fresh ingredients," he said, "and the presentation's nice. And it goes without saying that they're miles ahead in atmosphere. But whoever's doing the cooking has a few things to learn and a couple more to forget."

"Would you like to work in a place like that?"

"I've had a stint or two in fancier places. You know, upscale big city joints with a whole crew in the kitchen. I was way down in the pecking order, but even if I'd been higher up, I don't think I would have liked it. I'm happier behind the counter in a place like Kalamata, where nobody's likely to send back the wine because they don't like the way the cork smells."

"You can't get wine in Andy's, can you?"

"There you go," he said. "They can't send back what they can't order in the first place."

It was a weeknight, and the little theater was two-thirds empty. The film starred Jeff Bridges as a country singer who'd seen better days. There was a woman who thought she could save him, and he sat in his seat and saw himself and Carlene up there, playing out their parts.

Twenty minutes in, he reached over and took her hand.

He was still holding it when they rolled the final credits.

Outside, the air didn't feel like Montana. More like the Gulf Coast, humid and sultry. They walked toward her car, commented on the film they'd just seen, then fell silent. When they got to her car she turned to him and sighed and let her shoulders drop.

He said, "Before you drop me off, I'd love to see your house."

She turned, opened the door, got behind the wheel. Her house was on the edge of town, and neither of them spoke on the way there. She parked in the driveway, led him to the front door, unlocked it with a key.

Inside, he waited to embrace her until she'd closed the door. They stood kissing for a long time, and then she said, "Oh Jesus God," and took hold of his hand and led him to the bedroom at the rear of the house.

The double bed was made, with floral sheets and a tufted white bedspread. She drew the spread down, let it fall to the floor. Then she looked at him, her face slightly flushed, and took a breath, and pulled her dress over her head. She gave him a moment to look at her, then stepped forward and turned so that he could unhook her bra.

*   *   *

When she'd dozed off, he slipped out of the bed and got dressed. He had a hand on the doorknob when she said, "Wait."

"I'd better get on home," he said.

"You'll need a ride."

He said he didn't mind the walk. It would take him half an hour, she said, maybe more. And did he even know the route? She started to get up, but he put a hand on her shoulder and stopped her.

"I'll be fine," he said. "Get some sleep. I'll talk to you in the morning."

He hadn't been paying close attention on the ride to her house, but there weren't many turns and he'd always had a good sense of direction. He followed his instincts for ten or fifteen minutes, then came to a street he knew and had no trouble covering the remaining mile or so to Mrs. Minnick's house.

Spent the time recalling the warmth, the sweetness, the passion, the memories providing good company on the walk through the summer air, the sultry summer air.

The thought came to him that he could stay right here forever. And he wondered what he meant by that. Stay where? On these streets, walking back to his rooming house? In this town? With this woman?

Upstairs, in his bed, he wondered how long it would take to stuff everything he owned in the world into his carry-on. He'd bought a couple of things since he got off the Trailways coach. Would everything fit?

Funny thought to be thinking, at a time when he'd never felt so good. *Everything you ever wanted*, he thought. And was there anything on earth as dangerous as getting everything you ever wanted?

As soon as the breakfast rush died down, he called her at the library. It was a brief conversation, but served to make it clear that neither of them regretted the previous night, and both looked forward to more of the same. He suggested dinner on the following night, and she said she'd pick him up.

He was waiting out front, and got in beside her when she braked to a stop. She asked where he'd like to go for dinner, and something stopped him from answering, and there was a moment when the silence stretched. But it was not an awkward silence.

At length she said, "Are you hungry?"

"Not really."

She waited for him to fasten his seat belt, then pulled away from the curb. Neither of them said anything for two or three blocks, and then what she said was, "The only thing I'm hungry for right now is your cock."

She was looking straight ahead when she said it, and she went on looking straight ahead, her eyes on the road, both hands on the wheel.

He reached to cover one of her hands with his.

"I said that out loud, didn't I?"

"Either that or I've started hearing things."

"It's not like me," she said, "to talk like that."

"Well, I'm no expert, but it seemed like a perfectly good sentence to me. Grammatically correct and all."

" 'She was a slut, Your Honor, but she spoke proper English.' But, you know, it's the truth."

"That may be," he said. "Later on, though, you'll probably feel like a sandwich."

Her laughter was sudden, and rich. "Oh, that was just the right thing for you to say, Bill. It really and truly was. Bill?"

"What?"

"It's okay for me to be me, isn't it?"

*   *   *

In bed the novelty hadn't worn off but the anxiety was gone, and he found her a bold and eager lover, giving and taking pleasure with gusto. Afterward, as he'd predicted, her appetite for food returned. She told him to stay where he was, and he closed his eyes for a moment and drifted off, waking up when she came back with two plates of scrambled eggs and link sausages and bacon.

"Breakfast served at all hours," she announced. "Not as good as what you dish up every morning, I don't suppose."

He assured her the meal had nothing to apologize for.

They went back to bed, back to each other, and they talked idly while they pleasured one another. It had been such a long time, she told him, and he said it had been a long time for him, too. He answered her unspoken question by saying he hadn't been with anybody since he'd arrived in Montana.

"God, the responsibility," she said. "Representing my state. You know the motto?"

He didn't.

" 'Oro y plata.' Isn't that wonderful? 'Gold and silver.' Well, that's what prompted them to settle the place, but still. It strikes me as pretty crass when the best thing you can think of to say about your state is what you can dig out of it. Bill? Am I any good at it?"

"Good at—"

"You know. I hardly did anything before I got married. And, you know, it wasn't much of a marriage."

After it ended, she told him, there'd been nothing for a while, and then a brief affair with a married man. She'd actually liked that he was married, because it limited their meetings to brief encounters once or twice a week, which was all she wanted from him. But he never got over feeling guilty about their affair, and when he told her one time too many that what they were doing was wrong, she agreed with him and told him they ought to end it.

"He was shocked," she said, "although he tried to hide it. He thought it was my job to ease his conscience. But I think he was probably relieved when it was over. I know I was."

Then there had been a salesman from Eugene, Oregon who'd passed through, selling software to libraries. He took her to dinner and to bed, and she had a reasonably good time but never expected to see him again.

Nor did she, but a month or so later another fellow walked into the library and stopped at her desk. Not to sell software, or anything else, but to say Ed Carmichael had said he should stop by and give her his regards. She said that was nice, and he said it looked as though he was stuck in Cross Creek overnight, he'd just booked himself a motel room, and was there a decent place to eat in town? Say someplace where you could get a decent steak? And would she save him from having to dine alone?

She had dinner with him, and she had a couple of drinks, which she almost never did, and then she went back to his motel with him. Afterward he was enough of a gentleman to throw his clothes on and drive her back to the library, where she'd left her car. She drove home and spent more than the usual amount of time under the shower. She didn't feel dirty, not exactly, but she didn't feel entirely clean, either.

One week later somebody called her at the library. He was a friend of Ed's, or maybe he was a friend of Ed's friend, whose name she'd managed to forget. And he was in town, and Ed or Ed's friend had been talking about this fabulous steak dinner he'd had, but nobody could remember the name of the restaurant, and he wondered if maybe she was free that evening and—

"And I don't know what got into me, but what I said was his friend gave me the world's worst dose of gonorrhea, and if he really wanted I'd be more than happy to pass it on to him. And I'll never know what he would have said to that because I hung up on him."

"He's probably still trying to come up with a good line."

"All I knew," she said, "was I didn't want to be that girl. The one you call if you find yourself stuck in Cross Creek, Montana, and you buy her a steak and a couple of drinks, and you're home free. There may not be anything wrong with that girl, and she's probably having as good a time as the girl next door who collects Hummel figurines or the one down the block who rescues cats, but all the same I just knew she wasn't what I wanted to be."

"And here I am," he said, "stuck in Cross Creek, Montana."

"Here you are," she agreed, and laid a hand on him, as if to make sure of his presence. "First time I saw you, I thought, well, he'll wind up with the waitress."

"Who, Helen? I don't think—"

Helen was an aunt of Andy's who'd started waiting tables for something to do after her husband died. Carlene rolled her eyes, said, "I was thinking of the other one."

"I figured you meant Francie. Not my type, and you're just asking for trouble if you start up with a waitress."

"I think you're right. You're much better off with a librarian."

Besides, Francie was taken. He'd stood behind enough counters to know when a waitress was sleeping with the boss, and the first time he saw Andy and Francie make a point of not looking at each other, he'd put two and two together. He never said anything, or let on that he knew anything, and one night after he'd been at Kalamata a few months it was just him and Andy putting the diner to bed for the evening, and Andy felt like talking.

He almost said something now, to Carlene. Decided not to.

End of the week, Andy had an unusual expression on his face when he handed him his pay envelope. Not quite a smile, but close to it. He raised his own eyebrows, and Andy's smile widened.

"Better check it," he said. "Felt a little heavy to me."

He counted, and it was heavier by twenty-five dollars. He'd had a raise earlier, around the same time he started paying his rent by the month, and Andy had explained it as a sign of appreciation. It was, he assured him, no more than he deserved.

And now another raise. "Very generous," he told his boss. "Thank you."

"You've been good for the place, Bill. The goulash was your idea and your recipe. You rang it in as a daily special, and within a week we were getting requests for it, and now it's on the daily menu. People like it, and I can understand why."

"It's better now that we've got the right paprika."

"Maybe so, but there was nothing wrong with it in the first place. And the rhubarb pie. Not just thinking of it, but charming Mrs. Parkhill into trying her hand at it."

Hilda Parkhill was a rawboned widow who'd delivered two pies a day to the diner. One was always pecan and the other was usually apple.

"I just told her how much I missed my mother's rhubarb pie."

"Now she's selling us two pies one day and three the next, so it's good for her, and we're selling more pie than we used to, and you know what else? There's an interesting thing about the rhubarb pie, and I bet you know what it is."

"People usually order it a la mode."

"Like nine times out of ten. And if it doesn't occur to them, all it takes is a suggestion. 'You want a scoop of vanilla with that?' And they always do."

"Well, the rhubarb's tart, and the ice cream sets it off nicely."

"It's good from a food standpoint, and it's even better from a business standpoint. Can I ask you a question?"

"Go ahead."

"Did your mother really make rhubarb pie? I didn't think so. Bill, the raise is for the goulash and the rhubarb pie and all those scoops of vanilla, and if you keep on fattening up the population of Cross Creek, the next thing we'll do is open up a Weight Watchers chapter. Make money both ways, coming and going."

The first time he spent the night at Carlene's was on a Wednesday. She'd always offer to drive him home, and more often than not he'd choose to walk, but sometimes the weather or his own tiredness would lead him to accept the ride. This time she pointed out that he didn't have to be anywhere in the morning, so why not stay? He said he'd been thinking that himself.

He heard her alarm clock but decided to give himself a few more minutes, and fell back asleep. It was almost ten when he woke a second time, and she was long gone. A note on the kitchen table said there was fresh coffee in the pot, and invited him to help himself to breakfast.

All he wanted was coffee, and he drank two cups of it, sitting at the kitchen table and feeling both at home and out of place. He pictured himself going through the rooms, opening dresser drawers, checking the closets. But he never left the kitchen, and when he'd emptied the coffee pot he took it apart and washed it, washed his cup.

He started walking home, then changed his mind and walked to the library. It was far enough from her house that she always took her car, and on the way he decided it was time to go ahead and get that Montana driver's license. He had a good job, he had a girlfriend, it was about time he got himself a car.

Her face lit up when he entered the library, and he liked that the sight of him could elicit that sort of response. She put a lid on it, greeting him as *Mr. Thompson*. He neared the desk, and she dropped her voice and said he was sleeping so nicely she couldn't bear to wake him.

He moved away to look for a book, then eased over to the computer station. Only one of the four units was taken, a young mother consulting a medical website, and he seated himself diagonally opposite her and hit a few keys. All he knew about the Internet was you used Google and went where it led you, and that's what he did.

He Googled "William Jackson" and got a few million hits. He made the search more specific—"William Jackson + Galbraith North Dakota". The first item that came up told him that Rear Admiral William Jackson Galbraith was born on 15 September 1906 in Knoxville, Tennessee, and he could have read on to find out how North Dakota entered into it, but that was already more than he needed to know about the man.

This was more complicated than he thought.

But he pressed on and got the hang of it. The two cities of size near Galbraith were Fargo and Grand Forks, and it was a bus from Fargo that had brought him from Galbraith to Cross Creek. Galbraith didn't have a daily paper, but both those cities did, and both papers had subscribers in Galbraith. Both papers had websites, too—for Christ's sake, even the Cross Creek Public Library had a website—and he checked to see what he could learn from the *Grand Forks Herald* and the *Fargo Forum*.

Not much. You could enter a search, but it wasn't like going to their office and looking through back issues of the newspaper.

He'd figured out the date, the day he got on the bus, and he entered that, but that didn't really get him anywhere. You'd think it would show him the newspaper for that day, but it didn't, and what it did show him was about as useful to him as the fact that Admiral W. J. Galbraith was born in 1906 in wherever it was. Nashville? No, Knoxville, and wasn't his life richer for knowing that?

It would be easier if he knew what the hell he was doing. But he had to figure it out for himself, because it wasn't something someone could help him with. *I want to know if anybody was murdered in*

*Galbraith, North Dakota, on the 24th of April. I want to know if they
know who did it, and if it's a guy named Jackson.*

No, better not.

"North Dakota Murders."

That was better, better still when he added the year to the search
term.

He scrolled through the entries, clicked on some and scanned
them quickly, then returned to the list. Nothing in Galbraith, nothing
about a man named William Jackson.

He thought about his last morning in Galbraith. Waking up suddenly, flung abruptly into consciousness. Sprawled facedown on his
bed, still wearing all his clothes, even his shoes.

His shirt torn, ragged at the cuffs.

Scratches on his hands.

And ten or twelve hours gone. Some of them would have been
passed in sleep, or whatever you wanted to call the unconscious state
he'd been in. But the last thing he remembered—

The last thing was walking into a bar. He'd already been to two bars.
First to Kelsey's, where he dropped in for a drink more days than not,
and then to Blue Dog, where he went now and then, when Kelsey's
failed to take the edge off. During all his time in Galbraith, he'd made
no more than four or five visits to Blue Dog, and he'd never made it
out of there without having a drink too many. Once he'd been asked
to leave, but whatever he'd done couldn't have been too bad, because
he'd been welcome enough on his next visit.

Each time, though, he'd had enough to earn him a hangover the
next day, enough to poke Swiss cheese holes in his memory of the end
of the evening—getting home, unlocking the door, taking his clothes
off, putting himself to bed. He'd done all those things, and he remembered them, sort of. But the recollection was patchy, shifting its shape
when he tried to bring it into focus.

But this last time his head was clear when he left Blue Dog. Nobody asked him to leave. It was his idea, and he never even considered going home. There was another bar on the next block, one he'd passed dozens of times without once crossing the threshold. It looked a little low-rent, he'd always thought. A little shady.

What the hell was its name? A woman's name. Maggie, Maggie's something or other.

Time he paid them a visit. He remembered running that phrase through his mind.

And what else did he remember?

Precious little. Opening the door, and the smell hitting him in the face. The smell was of a couple of kinds of smoke, wrapped up in spilled beer and shirts worn too many times between washings. It was a long way from being a pleasant smell, was in fact distinctly unpleasant, and yet there was something comforting about it. Embracing him, drawing him in. *You belong here,* it seemed to assure him. *Come right on in. You're home.*

The bartender was a tall blonde with a hard face. She was wearing a pink blouse, entirely unbuttoned in front, showing a lacy black bra.

Maggie's Turn—that was the name of the place. Was she Maggie? Maybe, but probably not. Maggie had probably lost the joint in a crap game, or sold up and gone prospecting in the Yukon, or turning tricks in Ybor City. If there ever was a Maggie. Maybe the bar's name was the title of a song, rock or country, it could be either one.

He didn't remember ordering a drink, but he must have, because he remembered her pouring it, remembered picking it up, remembered bringing it to his lips.

And remembered absolutely nothing after that until he came suddenly awake, like a radio switched on at full volume. Wide awake, still in his clothes, still wearing his shoes, and possessed with the certain knowledge that something had gone terribly wrong.

*　　*　　*

Except it looked as though nothing had. Nothing bad enough to make newspaper headlines, nothing to make William Jackson a wanted man.

His shirt has been torn, with a couple of buttons gone. That could easily be the result of a bar fight, and not necessarily much of a fight at that. A little pushing and shoving, a hand making a fist around the bunched-up fabric of his shirt, tugging enough to rip the fabric and send a button flying.

Scratches on his hands.

He'd looked at them and imagined those hands around a woman's throat. And her smaller hands, clawing at him, until the strength went out of them.

Not a memory, nothing of the sort. Just his imagination, taking in the evidence, fabricating an explanation for it.

But his hands showed scratches more often than not. He used them at work, he grabbed this and reached for that all day long, and he was forever picking up something too hot or scraping a hand against one thing or another. For all he knew the scratches on his wrists and the backs of his hands had been there before he went into Kelsey's, and thus long before he got to Maggie's Turn. He could walk around with scratches on his hands without ever taking notice of them.

Not until he woke up with jagged holes in his memory, and pure dread for what might have filled them.

But a few scratches didn't mean his skin was under somebody's fingernails. And how could he have choked someone to death without raising enough of a stir to register on the Internet?

Was there a way to clear his searches from the computer's history? He was fairly certain there was, but he couldn't figure it out, and decided it wasn't important. He logged out, stood up.

Time to get on with his life.

*   *   *

That afternoon he filled out forms, showed his growing collection of ID, and applied for a Montana driver's license. The clerk established that he'd had an out-of-state license and said if he could show it he wouldn't have to take a road test. He explained that it had expired, and long enough ago that he hadn't even held on to it. He made an appointment for the road test.

There'd be a written test as well, and they gave him a booklet so he could study for it. He glanced at the booklet and saw that he could have taken the test on the spot, and without reading the booklet. A sample question: *True or false, in a three-lane highway the middle lane is used for parking.*

He'd made his appointment for three in the afternoon, a dead time at Kalamata. You needed to show up in a car for the road test, and somebody had to drive you there because you didn't have a license yet. He didn't want to ask Carlene to miss work, and Andy was out, as at least one of them had to be there to flip burgers.

"You'll take my Toyota," Andy said. "Francie'll run you there and bring you back. When we close tonight you and me'll take it out for a spin, give you a chance to get familiar with it. Every car's got things in a different place, the lights and the wipers and all, and you don't want to take a driving test with a car you never drove."

Andy sat beside him as he guided the car through the streets of Cross Creek, then here and there on state and county roads. "You won't have trouble," Andy assured him. "It's like swimming, riding a bicycle. The memory gets into your muscles and you can't forget. You could do it in your sleep."

"Some people do."

"Jesus, you think you're kidding," Andy said, and talked about a time when he'd fallen asleep at the wheel. "Drifted off the road, knocked down a road sign and clipped a telephone pole. Pretty much coasted into it, and it was a good thing I wasn't going fast, and an even better thing I pulled to the right instead of the left. It was a two-lane, runs north to Willard, and I could as easily have driven straight into oncoming traffic. So you never know, do you?"

When the time came, Andy tossed him the set of keys while Francie hung her apron on a peg. In the car she asked him was he nervous, and he said he wasn't. "I would be," she said. "You tell me something's a test, right away I'm all nerves. You got a car picked out, Bill?"

"Not yet."

"Andy's been talking about getting a pickup. You wanted, he'd give you a good price on this one."

He said it was something to think about. He pulled up at the building where he'd applied for the license, took the written test, and waited while a woman checked his answers and congratulated him on a perfect score. "Well, I was up all night studying," he said, and when she gave him a look he asked if anybody ever failed it.

"You'd be surprised," she said.

He returned to the car, and Francie drove him to the crossroads where they gave the road test. There were some folding chairs set up, and she sat and waited while a rail-thin man in a sort of generic khaki uniform had him drive here and there on back roads, going forward, backing up, making a three-point turn, and otherwise demonstrating that he knew the difference between an automobile and a sewing machine.

"Oh, hell, that's enough," the man said. "Most everybody passes, the average kid's done so much country driving by the time he gets here that he knows what to do. The ones from the Res, well, they don't need Montana's permission to drive on their own land, and when they want to be able to drive in the rest of the world, the only way they'll flunk the test is if they show up half in the bag. Which, I have to say, they sometimes do. You're okay, Mr. William M. Thompson. They call you Bill? Well, welcome to Montana's rolling highways, Bill."

*   *   *

So just like that he had a car and a license. There was no reason he could think of not to buy the car from Andy, who told him he could have it at ten percent below the dealer buy price quoted in the Blue Book, and that he could pay for it in weekly deductions from his pay.

He could have paid cash for it, he'd gone on adding to the stash in the money belt, but he decided to split the difference, paying Andy half and arranging to have his pay docked for the rest.

"You've been saving your money," Andy said.

"Well, what am I gonna spend it on?"

"Not too much in Cross Creek. Of course you want to take your lady out for a nice meal now and then. Presents for Christmas and her birthday, and God help you if you forget Valentine's Day. Flowers or candy, and if you're smart it'll be flowers *and* candy."

Had he ever mentioned Carlene? Not that he could recall. Still, it was a pretty small town. It figured that everybody would know everything.

"I'll keep that in mind," he said.

"And while you're at it, thank God and the angels that you've only got one birthday to remember and one woman to send flowers to. Ah, don't get me started. Saving your money, Bill, that's a good thing. Time might come when you might want to make a little investment."

"Oh?"

"Never mind. We'll save that for another day."

That night he took Carlene to the Conestoga. She made more of a fuss over his car than it deserved, and he pointed out that it wasn't exactly a Cadillac.

"But it's a car," she said, "and it's yours, and that's exciting. When was the last time you owned a car?"

Back in April, he thought. He'd driven into Galbraith in an aging

Buick, put a few bucks into transmission work while he was there, replaced two of the tires. And left it behind when he carried his suitcase to the Trailways station, because if they were looking for William Jackson the Buick would be something to key on.

When had he last owned a car? Well, technically, he probably still owned that Buick. It was a good bet they weren't looking for him, since he hadn't left a body behind in Galbraith, but he certainly wasn't going back for the car, and wondered idly who had it now. Wasn't a bad car, really. Burned oil, but you had to expect that.

What he said was, "Oh, it's been a while."

He'd picked her up at the library, and stopped there so that she could get her car, then followed her back to her place. He wasn't really in the mood and would have just as soon gone on home himself, but he didn't think that would go down too well.

And he wound up in the mood soon enough. "There's something I read about," she said, avoiding his eyes, and went on to do things that suggested a fruitful apprenticeship in a bordello in Port Said.

He drove to Kalamata. There were four parking places behind the diner, and Andy, who walked to and from work, had kept the Toyota in one of them for as long as he'd owned it. "The spot goes with the car," he'd said. "You get all the comforts of home with Mrs. Minnick, but what you don't get is a place to park."

He left the car in his spot, walked home, then remembered he was just about due for another bottle of Old Crow. At two ounces a day, a pint was gone in eight days. Lately he'd begun buying fifths instead, and a fifth was twenty-six ounces and change, so it lasted him that much longer. But there was just one drink left in the bottle, and a little less than a full drink at that, so he kept on until he was standing at the bar of the Stockman.

Without asking, the bartender reached for a fifth of Old Crow, then paused before slipping it into a paper sack. "Got a special on J. W. Dant," he said. "Generally more expensive than Crow by a dollar a bottle, and somebody decided that this months it's three dollars cheaper."

While he thought about it, the bartender set up a shot glass and filled it from a J. W. Dant bottle. "On the house," he announced, "so you can make an informed decision."

He picked it up, drank it down. "Tastes the same as the Old Crow."

"All you miss out on," the bartender said, "is that slick-looking bird on the label."

He nodded, and the man put the Old Crow back on the shelf and slipped the Dant into the paper sack.

He paid for the bottle, reached for his change, then stopped himself. He ordered another shot of the Dant, and stood there looking at it for a long moment before he picked it up and drank it down. Then he ordered another.

And that, he decided, was enough. He'd had enough to feel it, and he did feel it, and it wasn't a bad feeling. But it was as good as he needed to feel, and as much as he needed to drink, and he walked home carefully, used his key carefully, climbed the stairs carefully.

He put the bottle away, and now he had two bottles in the drawer, and that wouldn't do. There was less than a full drink in the Old Crow bottle, and it occurred to him that he probably ought to finish it now, so that he could get rid of the empty bottle in the morning.

Decided it could wait. Decided the dresser's bottom drawer, which no one but he himself ever opened, could hold two whiskey bottles for another day or two, and was better equipped to do so than he was to hold another slug of bourbon.

But there was something else to tend to before he got into bed.

He fetched his money belt, went through the bills and found his

North Dakota driver's license. It bore his photograph, along with the name of William M. Jackson. He pulled out his new Montana license and compared the two pictures, and decided that they looked more like each other than either of them looked like him.

He'd retained the North Dakota license in case he ever needed it for an emergency. If he'd had to drive, it was at least a valid license, with a couple of years to go before it would expire.

You couldn't tear it up, it was some sort of laminate of plastic and cardboard, and while it would probably burn, it might raise a stink in the process. He spent twenty minutes using his Swiss army knife's scissors to cut the thing into tiny fragments. The license resisted cutting, and it was hard to get leverage on the little scissors, and by the time the job was done to his satisfaction, he felt as sober as he'd been when he first walked into the Stockman.

In the bathroom, before he readied himself for bed, he flushed away the innumerable shreds of his old license. In bed, during the few minutes he waited for sleep to come, he thought that he had everything a man could need. He had a job and a place to live, he had a girlfriend who was good company in and out of bed, he had a car and a place to park it and Montana's official permission to drive it wherever he wished.

Everything a man could need.

He woke up with a headache and a dry mouth. But his memory was crystal clear. He wondered at some of what he recalled. Why had a quick stop to pick up a bottle of whiskey turned into three drinks in quick succession?

No answer to that, but no harm, either. Two glasses of water got rid of his thirst, and as many aspirin did the same for his headache.

Checked himself in the mirror, saw the same face he always saw. No better, no worse.

Off to greet the day.

A week later he worked the breakfast shift by himself, and Andy came in at lunchtime. When the noon rush faded, Andy said, "You know something, Bill, you got me thinking."

"Oh?"

"About pie. About pecan pie, specifically."

"There's a piece or two left, if you want one."

"How you got me started," Andy said, "is rhubarb pie and vanilla ice cream. Every time I sell a piece of pie, I ask, 'How about a scoop of vanilla ice cream with that?' And with rhubarb the answer is usually yes, and with the other pies it's sometimes yes and sometimes no. It's yes enough of the time to make it worth asking, but it's not the same as with the rhubarb."

"Well, there's a natural affinity, I guess."

"Affinity. I guess there is, and that's where I'm going with this. I'm thinking I'll start carrying a new flavor of ice cream, and can you guess what it is? Butter pecan."

"For the pecan pie."

"You don't think that rings the bell for affinity?"

"I'm just trying to figure how they'd taste together," he said. "Not bad, would be my guess, but what bothers me is the sound."

"The sound?"

"Pecan and butter pecan," he said.

Andy considered, nodded. "Like an echo."

"Well, sort of. Like a double dose of the same flavor, but there's no question you're on to something. Rhubarb and vanilla, pecan and what?" He'd known right away, but took his time coming up with it. "Oh," he said, "I bet that would work."

"What's that?"

"It's just an idea, but I'm thinking rum raisin."

" 'One pecan pie coming up, and how about a scoop of rum raisin with that?' Oh, I like that. I can just about taste it. You ever try it yourself?"

"I haven't got much of a sweet tooth, Andy."

"No, come to think of it, I don't recall ever seeing you eating pie *or* ice cream. But you're a genius at knowing what goes with what. You know what else I like about it? They're already feeling pretty daring ordering a rich dessert, and now they get to top it off with something that sounds like drinking. You happen to know if there's any actual rum in rum raisin?"

"It's probably just rum flavoring, wouldn't you think?"

"Well, I don't suppose you need a liquor license to sell it. It's just that there'll be some of them who'll have to know. There's these four women come in every Wednesday after they work on their quilts over at the First Methodist. You know the ones I mean?"

He nodded. "Always take a booth."

"And generally the same booth every time, and when I remember I save it for 'em. 'Now one of you young ladies better have vanilla, and be the designated driver.' "

"You've got your lines all worked out."

"What I'll do, I'll call in an order right now before I forget. Rum raisin ice cream. Have to wonder how the Mormons feel about it, and I guess we'll find out, won't we? Oh, we're gonna have some fun, Bill. And you know what else? We're gonna sell us some ice cream."

*   *   *

Later that week he drove to Carlene's to pick her up, and she motioned him inside. As soon as he crossed the threshold his nostrils filled with cooking smells and he knew they weren't going anywhere.

She'd set the table with proper china and cloth napkins, and she made him sit while she filled two plates in the kitchen and brought them to the table.

It was a Belgian-style beef stew, with the cubes of beef cooked in beer, along with potatoes and root vegetables. She'd done the prep work the night before, then switched on the slow cooker before she left for work.

"It's very frightening," she said, "to prepare an elaborate meal for a man who cooks for a living. But it's good, isn't it?"

It was delicious, and he told her so. She'd bought three bottles of the beer, a dark German brew, and only used one in the stew, and they each drank a beer with the meal. Later they shared the sofa and watched TV and wound up in bed. Their lovemaking was slow and gentle, and then passion took hold of both of them.

Afterward he caught himself dozing off, and started to get up. She said, "Don't, you're tired."

"They'll see my car."

"So? It's a perfectly nice car. It's nothing to be ashamed of."

"I meant—"

"I know what you meant, and do you really think we're likely to shock anybody? Everybody knows we're an item."

"An item."

"We can decide what to call it in the morning."

And in the morning, without raising the subject of what to call whatever they had, she suggested he might want to keep a change of clothes at her house. And, oh, a spare razor. That sort of thing.

He had a shower, put his clothes back on. Drank a cup of coffee.

*   *   *

It had been six weeks since he bought Andy's Toyota, and he'd been wondering when they'd have that conversation about an investment he might want to consider. He was in no rush, but he knew it was coming.

Cross Creek got snow flurries one evening, and then two days later the first snow of the season fell overnight and melted in the morning sunlight. That gave the breakfast crowd a topic of conversation, and everybody had something to say about it, none of it very interesting.

When the room had mostly cleared, Andy drew two mugs of coffee and gave a nod to Helen, who took it as signal to take his place behind the counter. "Come on," he said to Bill. "Want to talk with you."

When they were seated across from each other in a back booth, he said, "Conversation I been having with you in my head for months now, and it's time I came out and let you know what I've been thinking. Though you can probably guess."

"Just so you're not about to fire me."

"Yeah, building up my courage." He sipped his coffee. "The hell, you have to know where this is going. I been running this place all my life, it feels like, and I'm not getting any younger, and if there's anything I want to do in my life, it's getting to be time to do it."

"Like that trip to Paris."

"Which is never gonna happen, except it might, except how could it if I'm running this joint? You see where this is going."

"I guess I do."

"What keeps me here is what am I gonna do, lock the doors and drop the keys in the storm drain? I suppose I could do just that. This town's been good to me, and same for the people who eat here and the ones who work here, but that doesn't mean I owe anybody anything but a fair wage or a good meal. And if Kalamata closes, who's gonna go hungry?"

Andy was looking off to one side, looking at nothing but the past and the future. Looking for words, Bill thought, and gave him time to find them.

"You spend your life running a joint, do you want to walk away from it? Well, you do and you don't. You want to leave it in good hands."

Silence again, and his turn to break it. "I have a feeling you're not talking about Helen or Francine."

"It's a good business, Bill. It's fed me and mine for a lot of years, and put clothes on our backs, and I have to say it's as recession-proof as a funeral home. People gotta eat. They may cut back on the high-ticket joints, but they'll still show up for their eggs over easy." His face softened. "And their goulash," he said. "And their rhubarb pie."

"With a scoop of vanilla," he said. "Andy, you said it yourself, it's a good business. Which means it's worth money, which means you can't give it away."

"No, I'd need to sell it."

"And that's only right, and if I had the money—"

"Could you get your hands on twenty-five hundred dollars?"

He had a little over twice that in the money belt.

"Say I could. What would that buy me? The coffee urns and a couple of counter stools? Jesus, besides the building you own the structure, the real estate."

Andy held up a hand to stop him. "I been talking to my accountant," he said, "and it works. You'll pay me out of your receipts. Twenty-five hundred down and the rest according to a formula. I forget how many years you'll be paying me off, but in the meantime you'll be making a decent living, and at the end of the rainbow it's all yours, free and clear."

"Jesus," he said.

"Now what you want to do is think about it, Bill. It's not like I want to go home and start packing. I figure I want one more Montana winter so I don't forget what they're like, so we got plenty of time for you to decide and for the accountant to work out the details and the lawyer to put the paperwork together. But what I'd love to do is shake your hand sometime in May or June, and once that's done, you're the owner and proprietor of Kalamata."

"It's a lot to think about."

"Of course it is—or it's a no-brainer, depending how you look at it. Incidentally, Kalamata. No reason you can't change the name to something you like."

"What would I change it to?"

"Well, half the town calls it the Calamity. You could change the sign and make it official."

"What everybody calls it," he said, "is Andy's."

"And they'll keep on calling it that for the first year or two, and then it'll be Bill's, and pretty soon not one person in ten'll remember it was ever anything else. Jesus, I'm getting choked up, and it's a fucking diner is all it is. A diner I'll be glad to walk away from, and the day you cooked that first omelet, what came into my head is maybe this is the guy who'll take the place off my hands. So you think about it, okay?"

He thought about it off and on for three days. Then he told Carlene.

They were on her couch eating pizza in front of her TV, and she just listened while he recounted Andy Page's offer. She was very good at listening, at giving a person room to talk, and that was one of the things he particularly appreciated about her.

When he finished, she remained silent for a moment, and then what she said surprised him. She asked him if he'd change the name.

"I don't know," he said. "Do you think I should?"

"I guess that depends on how much you'd change the place itself."

"How?"

"I don't know. Would you redecorate? Redo the menu?"

"It wouldn't hurt to throw a coat of paint on the walls, but there's no rush, and it won't look that different afterward, just a little less shopworn. The menu, well, I've been making changes now and then, and I'd keep tweaking it, you know? I could take a couple of the Greek dishes off the menu. Pastitsio, most customers don't know what it is. Change it up and call it lasagna and I bet it'd move faster."

He told her some more of his ideas. She said, "You're excited about it."

"A little."

"And something else. What's holding you back?"

"Well, what do I know about running a restaurant?"

"A lot, I'd say."

"About cooking, and selling food. What do I know about being a boss?"

"You've watched Andy."

And a lot of other men over a lot of years. "You can only learn so much by watching," he said. "Hiring and firing, dealing with suppliers. It could be a headache."

"I guess it could."

"He was going nuts before I showed up. I could run the place the way he did, with just Francie and Helen, but I'd be working myself to death unless I found somebody."

"You'd put a sign in the window," she said, "and some handsome stranger would take one look at it and hop off the bus."

"Yeah, there you go. And I'd have to hope he spotted some equivalent of a hot librarian and decided to stick around. Andy makes decent money, but that's no guarantee that I would. I could go broke."

"And if you did?"

"I'd give the place back to him and get on the next bus."

"Or you could give the place back to him," she said, "and *not* get on the bus. But first you'd have to go broke, and I don't think that would happen. You're too good at what you do."

And a little later he said, "You know, maybe I'll hit the library tomorrow. Check out something on restaurant management."

He showed up mid-morning, browsed the business section and the food section, carried a couple of books over to a table, sat down and read. At one point he realized nothing he read was registering. The words just passed in front of his eyes and trailed off into the distance.

He re-shelved the books. You were supposed to leave them, on the premise that you couldn't be trusted to put them back in the right place, but he remembered where they'd come from and managed to put them where they belonged.

Went over to the computers. All four were unattended, and he sat down all by himself and logged on, did a little idle surfing. Checked out a few recipes for lasagna, which seemed to be a dish with infinite variations and no ironclad requirement beside big flat noodles, and for all he knew even that was negotiable.

Could be interesting. Try different recipes, find the one he liked the best, then play with the proportions and the seasoning until it was just the way he wanted it.

Other dishes he could experiment with as well, menu staples he'd learned to make the way Andy made them, but if it was his diner he could make his own rules.

Thought about William Jackson and Galbraith, North Dakota. But nothing had happened, he reminded himself. He'd left town, had felt the hot breath of the hound of hell on his neck even as the bus took him away from there, but it was all unnecessary, wasn't it?

If he thought about it clinically, it was just a fear, one that came to him automatically when drink left him with holes in his memory. If there was a span of time unaccounted for, he could only imagine the worst. He must have done something wrong, something unspeakable. Otherwise why would his memory insist on blocking it out?

And so he'd feared the worst, and acted accordingly. Pure unreasoning fear, based on nothing.

He drew a breath, held it for a moment.

And then he did something he hadn't done in longer than he could remember. Not since he got to Cross Creek, not once in Galbraith, nor in the town before Galbraith, or the one before that.

He called up Google, keyed "Walter Hradcany" into the search box. Hit *Enter*.

And the entries popped up, even after all the years. There were a slew of them, mostly in West Texas, but some more recent ones popped up on websites devoted to unsolved crimes. The stories they told differed in details, but not in their essentials. A young woman named Pamilla Thurston had been found strangled to death in the house trailer she had previously shared with her estranged husband. She'd been dead for 48 to 72 hours before her body was found.

Inevitably, suspicion centered upon the husband, but he held up under questioning, and so did his alibi. Pamilla had last been seen at a roadhouse just outside the town limits of Plainview, no more than two miles from her residence. She had been a regular patron, especially since her husband had moved out, and left with one man or another more often than not.

It was hard to determine which night had been her last, and hard for anyone to recall with certainty who'd been her companion on either of the possible final nights. Several names came up, and several men had the challenging task of proving that they hadn't gone home with Pamilla. But one man whose name came up was a short-order cook named Walter Hradcany. No one remembered seeing him leave the roadhouse with Pamilla, but two people recalled he'd been talking with her, so the Hale County cops went looking for him.

And found out he'd disappeared. One day he was there in Plainview and the next day he was gone. He was supposed to work the early shift at Grider's Family Restaurant, but he never showed and never called in. He'd been one of the permanent guests at a budget motel, paying by the week, and he'd left clothes in the dresser and toilet articles in the bathroom, and his car was still parked in front of his unit. It seemed possible that he was dead himself, murdered by the same person who'd killed Pamilla. Or he might have died by his own hand, wandered off into the middle of somebody's wheat field and shot himself.

His body never turned up. And the DNA they got from the hairs in his comb matched what they found under Pamilla's fingernails. So as far as local law enforcement was concerned, Walter Hradcany was more than a person of interest. They had enough on him to close the case, but they couldn't clear it, because they never turned up a trace of him.

A distinctive name, Walter Hradcany.

There had to be a way to clear the computer's history, and he looked for it until he found it. He erased everything for the past two days, and then he built up a little fresh history, searching once more for recipes and restaurant management tips.

Not that the Walter Hradcany search could be entirely expunged. He'd seen enough TV to know that anything you did on a computer left a spoor that lingered forever. On the hard drive, in Google's infinite files, or in some metadata base in Washington.

But they'd have to be looking hard to find it, and they'd need a reason, and they didn't have one. And he didn't intend to give them one, either.

*   *   *

The next day he opened up at Kalamata and served a lot of breakfasts. Around eleven he almost said something to Andy, but he let it go until the middle of the afternoon.

Then he said, "Well, I thought it over, and I could just as easy have answered you on the spot. It's a wonderful offer and I'd have to be crazy to say no to it. Only bad thing about it is I'll miss working alongside of you."

"And the only problem you'll have is finding a fry cook as good as the one I found. I'll get my guy to put something on paper, but that's just the formalities. Far as I'm concerned, we got ourselves a deal."

He spent the rest of his shift thinking of the computer search, thinking about Plainview, Texas. Out in the Panhandle, and the name fit; the only view you had out there was a view of the Plains.

Nice enough town.

Pamilla Thurston. He'd never known her last name, or the unusual way she spelled her first name. Still didn't have a clue how she'd pronounced it, same as if it was Pamela or to rhyme, sort of, with vanilla.

Pam, that's what people called her.

He couldn't really remember what she looked like. When he tried to picture her, the image that came to him was a blend of photographs he'd seen in the newspaper.

So what did he remember?

Talking to her, buying her a drink. He'd been wearing a string tie— well, it was West Texas, it was a cowboy bar. And she'd stepped in close and snugged up the turquoise slide, letting her body lean a little against his, giving him a nose full of her perfume.

That was all he remembered.

Until he woke up in his motel room, all his clothes on, including his boots. Sprawled on the bed, his feet trailing on the floor.

Nothing in his memory after she'd tightened his tie. Nothing in his head but the sure knowledge that something bad had happened.

He was on a northbound bus, and halfway to Lubbock he started to wonder if he'd lost his mind. Wake up with a bad feeling and skip town like a shot? Leave everything behind, even the car that would have been a lot more comfortable than the damn bus? All that because he was hungover bad enough to think something must have happened?

That was a few minutes before he was aware of the soreness in his forearms. Noticed the blood that had seeped through his shirtsleeves. Rolled up the sleeves, saw the scratches.

It wasn't until the following evening that he saw Carlene. He'd expected to tell her of his decision, but somehow kept letting the opportunity go by. They went to a movie, and his mind kept wandering from the story, rehearsing a conversation in his head. Then, by the time the film was over, he'd decided to let it ride.

But he didn't want her to hear it from someone else first, and news got around in Cross Creek. A day or two later he was looking for a way to ease into the subject, when she made it easy for him by asking if he'd decided yet.

"I think I probably decided the minute Andy popped the question," he said. "He called it a no-brainer, and he was right."

"Still, it's a big step. I'd say you were wise to take time to think it over. Well, congratulations, Mr. Restauranteur."

"Right. Next thing you know they'll give me a TV show, like what's his name."

"Emeril?"

"I was thinking of that guy who goes around the world eating bugs and worms."

"Anthony Bourdain. We've got several of his books in the library."

"Well, if I ever need to know how to cook a cockroach . . ."

"You'll know where to look. Honey, we should celebrate. This time I'll take you out to dinner. Tomorrow night?"

"Sure," he said. "That'd be great."

Their lovemaking was practiced but intense, and even as he took his pleasure he felt a wave of sadness roll in on him.

When her breathing slowed, he slipped out of bed and put his clothes on. He drove home, left his car in his spot at the diner, and walked on home.

The following evening he called her from Kalamata. He was feeling under the weather, he told her, and there was fresh snow on the ground with more of it in the forecast, and tomorrow or the next day would be a better choice for their festive dinner. He'd fix himself something before he left, then go home and make it an early night.

"Feel better," she told him.

There was a piece of pecan pie left, and he decided that would do him for dinner. He topped it with a scoop of rum raisin ice cream. It had turned out to be a successful combination, and had in fact upped the sales of both components, the pie and the ice cream.

And he could see why. They were a good match, the rum raisin and the pecan.

He could make the place work. Hell, it worked already, and his mind kept coming up with ways to make it better.

He walked home. There was snow on the ground, but the sidewalks were mostly cleared, and his shoes could handle a few inches of snow with no trouble. He let himself into Mrs. Minnick's house, stomped his shoes clean in the entryway, went up to his room. His coat was a heavy-duty Buffalo plaid from Walmart, all wool, all red and black squares, and once he'd hung it on a doorknob he retrieved the bottle of J. W. Dant from the bottom drawer.

It was a little more than a third full. He poured two ounces of whiskey into his drinking glass and moved his chair over to the window. It was peaceful, with a little snow on the ground, and of course it was quiet.

It suited him here, he thought. He'd slept well in this bed, in this room. It was so remarkably convenient to Kalamata that even now, when he owned a car, he never used it to get to and from work. The walk each morning got the blood moving in his veins and set him up for a day's work. The walk home each night gave him a chance to shed all the workday tension on the way.

Would he be able to stay?

Because it was perfectly appropriate for a new man in town, a fry cook, a counterman, to live in a furnished room. But he was no longer a new man in town, no longer a drifter who'd got off a bus and grabbed a job to support him while he figured out where to go next. He'd been there long enough for Cross Creek to know who he was, or at least who they thought him to be. He was Bill, worked alongside Andy at Kalamata, and maybe he ought to occupy living quarters that suited his station in life.

Not that there was anything less than respectable about Mrs. Minnick's.

Soon everybody would know he'd arranged to take over the diner. And not long after that he'd be its owner, and did a man who owned a restaurant live in a furnished room, however respectable it might be?

A man in that position ought to have an apartment. Ought to have a house, really.

He lifted the glass, found he'd drained it. He considered the fact, and then he walked to the dresser, where the bottle stood waiting. He'd left it standing on top of the dresser instead of returning it to the drawer, perhaps in anticipation of this moment.

He poured another two-ounce measure of bourbon into his glass and returned to the chair. He took the glass of whiskey with him, of course, and this time he took the bottle, too.

The bourbon fed his imagination, and he gave it free rein. Saw himself moving in with Carlene. Keeping his room but living with her, and the town would be fine with that, there were plenty of couples living together without being married. Cross Creek generally expected you to make it legal when there was a kid on the way, but even that was negotiable nowadays.

Still, living together that way would feel unresolved, and it wouldn't be long before he'd ask her to marry him, and even if she hadn't said anything along those lines, it would be what she was waiting to hear. He figured the wedding would be something simple, the two of them standing up in front of a town clerk or a justice of the peace, however it worked in Montana, or a minister if she wanted, because it didn't make any difference to him. Just the two of them, or maybe Andy to be his best man and a friend from the library to stand up for her, and whoever else she wanted to invite.

If there had to be something along the lines of a reception, Kalamata could cater it.

He went to refill his glass, found the bottle was empty. He must have poured a time or two without paying any real attention to what he was doing. He'd had what, eight or nine ounces of bourbon?

Didn't feel any different. Still comfortably tired, the way he always was at the end of a long day's work. Still feeling the lingering sadness that had come upon him during their lovemaking the night before; he'd gone to sleep with it and awakened with it, and it was still there.

Once they were married, they could sell her house. They'd buy something larger and more conveniently located, maybe one of the big old homes a half-mile or so east of the diner. If her house was a little snug for two people, those Victorians had far more space than the two of them needed. There'd be rooms they had no use for, rooms they'd have to furnish or leave empty.

A big kitchen, most likely. A formal dining room.

Maybe a sun parlor. A front porch, and possibly an upstairs porch as well.

Trees. A front lawn, a back yard.

Way more than either of them needed. Still, he'd always wanted a house like that. Couldn't say why, hadn't lived in anything that grand as a kid growing up. Never knew anybody in a house like that, not really.

Liked the way they looked, though. Just half a mile down Main, meant he could still walk home from the diner. Make himself a drink, take it out on the front porch. Sit in a rocker, sip his bourbon.

Two rockers, and she'd sit in the other one. The two of them, side by side, on their porch. He'd talk a little, about his day, and she'd do the same, and then they'd fall silent and just sit there, not needing to say anything, content to share the silence.

All a man could want. All he'd ever wanted, just waiting for him to say yes to it.

Outside it had resumed snowing. It wasn't working very hard at it. The big flakes were pretty as they fell through beams of light.

He sat there, watching, thinking. He looked at the empty glass, at the empty bottle.

He got to his feet.

*   *   *

By the time he'd crossed from the doorway to the bar, the Stockman's bartender had an unopened fifth of Dant in a paper bag. When he shook his head, the fellow said, "Back to Old Crow?"

"No, Dant's good, but I don't need a bottle. Just a drink."

"Neat?"

"With water back. And make it a double."

He picked up the glass and looked at it, then looked around the room. Football on the TV with the sound off, six or seven men in the room besides himself and the bartender. Familiar faces, most of them, but nobody he'd ever spoken to, no one he knew by name.

The drink was gone, the bartender was pouring him another, helping himself to the price of it from the change on the bar top.

The water glass was still full.

He drank the second double. He'd barely been aware of drinking the first one, but now he paid attention, took a moment to tune in to the alcohol in his system. But he couldn't feel it. He knew he'd had a lot to drink, could have come up with a total, but he didn't seem to be able to feel any of it. Not that he felt sober, but he didn't really feel drunk, either. All he felt was—what?

Couldn't find the word for it.

A commercial on the TV, someone pouring beer into a glass. The last beer he'd had was when Carlene cooked that Flemish pot roast, and the last beer before that was too long ago to remember. Nothing wrong with beer, but what was the point of it? If a man was going to drink, why drink anything but whiskey?

"Another?"

Why not?

*   *   *

Under the weather. That had been his excuse to Carlene, breaking their date. Outside, his fingers just the least bit clumsy with the buttons of his wool Walmart jacket, he told himself that there was plenty of weather to be under. Snow still falling, with a little wind blowing up to drive it.

He'd finished his third drink and said no to a fourth, and he stood in the snow and wondered which way to go. Turn right and walk back to Mrs. Minnick's. Turn left and then what?

Walk a block and a half, he thought, to Panama Red's. He'd never been there, but he knew it by reputation. What he'd heard, they got a rougher crowd.

Standing there, trying to decide. Turn left or turn right.

That was the last thing he remembered.

When his eyes snapped open he willed them shut before they had time to register an image. He tried to will consciousness away, but that didn't work. He was awake, like it or not.

And he was sprawled on the floor, one arm pinned awkwardly beneath him. He tried to learn what he could without opening his eyes, using his other senses in turn. He felt cold, and he felt pain mixed with numbness in one hand, its circulation cut off by his body weight. He smelled vomit, and he tasted blood in the back of his throat.

He heard nothing.

He didn't want to open his eyes for fear of what he'd see. But he was even more afraid to remain unknowing.

When he forced his eyes open he saw where he was, sprawled on his own floor. He moved slowly, got to his knees and then to his feet, swaying slightly as he breathed deeply and tried to get his balance.

He'd evidently made it back to his room, closed the door once he was inside. He'd sat on his chair, or tried to, and had managed to knock it over and break one of its legs on the way down.

He'd vomited. There was vomit on the rug, streaks of vomit on the front of the wool jacket. He was still wearing the jacket, but he'd managed to unbutton it before he sat down and passed out. Or he'd never gotten around to buttoning it when he headed for home.

No point trying to work it out now. No time to waste.

There was, thank God, nobody in the hallway. He went to the bathroom, cleaned himself up as well as he could. Washed his hands, his face. He'd bloodied his nose, or someone had bloodied it for him, and it hurt when he dabbed at it, but he didn't let the pain stop him. He dampened a towel and scrubbed at the stains on his jacket, and on the shirt beneath it.

Not too much blood on the jacket. More on the shirt beneath it, a long-sleeved polo shirt that had come with him from Galbraith. He didn't bother trying to clean it up, because there were other shirts he could wear, but in this weather he'd need the jacket.

Hurry up. Don't stop to think, no time to think. Later, later he could think all he wanted. More than he wanted, really.

Back to the room. Strip off the bloody shirt, toss it in the trash basket. Pull open drawers, prop his suitcase on the bed, stuff things into it. Take this, leave that, decisions made more by reflex than by thought. No time to waste, Jesus, no time to waste.

Take his drinking glass? Oh, Jesus, what did he need with that?

But he took it. And he retrieved the bloody shirt, found a plastic grocery sack to hold it, stuffed it in his bag.

The first bus was headed for Fargo, and that wasn't the direction he wanted to go. He made himself stay in the station, perched on a stool at the lunch counter. A lifetime ago Andy had assured him he'd be taking his life in his hands if he ate there, but the thought of eating anything anywhere was impossible. He sat with a cup of black coffee. It had started out weak and sat on the heating element until it had turned to sludge, and he drank it anyway and had a second cup.

He couldn't keep from watching the door, bracing himself every time it opened, waiting for someone to walk in with a badge. At one point a pair of uniformed deputies did come in, stepped to the counter and picked up a couple of coffees to go. They both ordered it with a lot of cream and sugar, and he wondered if that would help.

He'd finished a little less than half of his own second cup when his bus came, bound for Spokane.

He relaxed, but only a little, when the bus pulled out. If Cross Creek had a *Resume Speed* sign at the edge of town, he missed seeing it. It was snowing again, so it was easy to miss things.

Minnie Pearl's home town. Funny how a line like that would stay with you.

He closed his eyes, surprised himself by dozing off.

When he woke up they were still in Montana. He looked out the window and watched a freight train a few hundred yards north of the highway, running west at about the same speed as the bus. He found himself counting the cars, and he drifted off like that, and the next time his eyes opened they were in Idaho, coming into Coeur d'Alene. He didn't know how much difference it made, crossing from one state to another. It worked like a charm for Bonnie and Clyde, the boxy cop cars had to turn around and go home when they hit the state line, but things had changed some since then.

They stopped for fifteen minutes in Coeur d'Alene, with some passengers hopping off for a smoke break. He stayed where he was, and the bus pulled out on schedule, with half an hour to go before they were due in Spokane.

He'd never been to Spokane. Bigger city than he was used to, and that might make it easier to get lost in. Other hand, it was the right time of year to be heading someplace warm. Get off in Spokane, catch something southbound. There'd be towns all the way to the Mexican border, and they'd all have restaurants, and there was always a restaurant that needed somebody who knew his way around a grill.

Once he landed somewhere, he'd have to take that bloodstained shirt and lose it. He was pretty sure it was his own blood and nobody else's, because he'd evidently taken a pretty good punch in the nose, but his knuckles were bruised, so he'd very likely gotten in a few licks of his own.

Two drunks punch each other out in a barroom brawl, well, that was no way to get your picture on a post office wall. And if that's all it amounted to, why did he have to leave town? Why walk away from his room, his car, his job? His girlfriend?

There was every chance in the world no one was chasing him, just as no one had chased him out of Galbraith or the town before Galbraith. For Christ's sake, it was odds-on he hadn't been in a fight at all. Drunk as he was, he could have fallen down without getting a push.

Did he even make it to Panama Red's? Probably fell on his face before he got there, skinned his knuckles trying to break his fall, bloodied his nose, scrambled to his feet only to fall a couple more times on the way home, pausing to puke a time or two while he was at it. Then pulled himself together enough to get in the door and up to his room, and, well, the rest was clear enough. He couldn't remember it, but he could see a movie of it in his mind—the chair collapsing, the floor rushing up at him, the lights going out.

*　　　*　　　*

By the time he got off the bus in Spokane, he knew he wanted some-place hot and dry. Some town in the desert, California or Nevada or Arizona.

Make a nice change.

Trailways and Greyhound shared the terminal in Spokane, and a sleepy-eyed man at the Greyhound window sold him a ticket to Sac-ramento. That wasn't where he wanted to wind up, but he could get a room there for a couple of nights, then plan his way south from there.

In the washroom, he stuffed the bloody shirt, sack and all, into a trash container. It was good to be rid of it, and he wasn't worried some janitor would rush it to the CSI crime lab.

His own blood, he was sure of it. All he'd had to do was clean him-self up and he could have stayed in Cross Creek. Told Mrs. Minnick her chair just collapsed under him, said it was probably his own fault and paid to replace it. And if he'd been in a fight, if he'd made it to Panama Red's and raised a little hell there, well, when did that get to be a hanging offense? He was still good old Bill Thompson, decent respectable fellow, worked behind the counter at Andy's diner, and if once a year he got a wild hair and had himself a snootful, well, sheesh, man, it could happen to a bishop, you know?

He drank a cup of coffee, ate a dish of scrambled eggs and bacon. The coffee was so-so, and the eggs and bacon weren't as good as they'd have been if he'd cooked them himself, but at least he had an appetite and at least he was putting food in his stomach. He had a second cup of coffee and even thought about a piece of pie, but decided it would be too much of a disappointment after what he'd gotten used to.

If he'd stayed, if he'd gone ahead and bought Kalamata, he'd have had Edith Parkhill working nights and weekends. He'd have been sell-ing pie as fast as she could bake it. The woman had a gift.

*　　　　*　　　　*

He had to share a seat on the bus to Sacramento. His companion was an older man who mostly slept, and didn't snore too badly. He slept himself, and woke up thinking if he had any sense he'd change buses at the next opportunity and head back where he'd come from. Back to Cross Creek, back to the rooming house and the diner. Back to Carlene.

Except he couldn't.

Because he'd had to leave, and somewhere within himself he must have known that, or why break the date with Carlene? Why empty the bottle and go out for more?

Coming to, lying on the floor in a mess of blood and vomit, along with all the fear and all the dread and all the guilt, along with everything, there'd been another terrible thought.

Now's your chance. You can cut and run, you can leave it all behind.

Beside him, the old man shifted in his sleep, let out a sigh.

He let out a sigh of his own, thought again of how he'd been lying there in a pile of blood and puke.

Damned lucky he'd landed face down. You vomit while you're passed out, you could breathe it in, choke on it. Die without ever knowing what was happening.

And wouldn't that be a hell of a thing.

Lawrence Block has been writing award-winning mystery and suspense fiction for half a century. His newest book, a sequel to his greatly successful Hopper anthology *In Sunlight or in Shadow*, is *Alive in Shape and Color,* a 17-story anthology with each story illustrated by a great painting; authors include Lee Child, Joyce Carol Oates, Michael Connelly, Joe Lansdale, Jeffery Deaver and David Morrell. His most recent novel, pitched by his Hollywood agent as "James M. Cain on Viagra," is *The Girl with the Deep Blue Eyes*. Other recent works of fiction include *The Burglar Who Counted The Spoons*, featuring Bernie Rhodenbarr; *Keller's Fedora*, featuring philatelist and assassin Keller; and *A Drop Of The Hard Stuff*, featuring Matthew Scudder, brilliantly embodied by Liam Neeson in the 2014 film, *A Walk Among The Tombstones*. Several of his other books have also been filmed, although not terribly well. He's well known for his books for writers, including the classic *Telling Lies For Fun & Profit* and *Write For Your Life*, and has recently published a collection of his writings about the mystery genre and its practitioners, *The Crime Of Our Lives*. In addition to prose works, he has written episodic television (*Tilt!*) and the Wong Kar-wai film, *My Blueberry Nights*. He is a modest and humble fellow, although you would never guess as much from this biographical note.

Email: lawbloc@gmail.com
Twitter: @LawrenceBlock
Facebook: lawrence.block
Website: lawrenceblock.com

Made in the USA
Columbia, SC
16 January 2019